We cooled down slowly, all curled and sealed to each other, sticky and steamy and sweet-smelling. I traced the outline of her cheek and neck and shoulder; she tangled her hands wordlessly in my hair. We were silent, in fact, quiet as people in holy places, reverent, humbled, awed. But in my head, words rattled to break free, words like love and need, words that, I realized, despite all this, were far too risky and raw. I felt naked without them now, and thought of Elaine again; "I love you" was a kind of seal, a chant we used, that made our sex a sacrament.

I had lost all track of time, except that my body felt the kind of pleasured numbness I'd known only after hours of lovemaking. Zena Beth twitched once in my arms as she tripped into some dream. I lay there a long while, breathing in the scent of her scalp, straining in the dim light to admire her body. When I tried to roll over, she whimpered a little and clamped her arm tightly around me from behind. What a whole different language she spoke in her sleep, I marveled, and would it make any difference at all in the morning?

DIANE SALVATORE

Love, Zena Beth

NAIAD
1993

Printed in the United States of America on acid-free paper
First Trade Paperback Edition

Edited by Katherine V. Forrest
Cover design by Catherine Hopkins
Typeset by Sandi Stancil

Library of Congress Cataloging-in-Publication Data

Salvatore, Diane.
    Love, Zena Beth / By Diane Salvatore.
        p.   cm.
    ISBN 1-56280-030-2
    I. Title.
PS3569.A46234L6   1992
813′.54–dc20
                                                    92-12741
                                                        CIP

For "HB"

About the Author

Diane Salvatore has been a magazine editor for over ten years. Her first novel, *Benediction,* was nominated for a Lambda Literary Award as the best Lesbian Fiction of 1991.

— 1 —

I stood inside the door, wearing the hotel's white terry cloth robe, watching Zena Beth Frazer in the hallway as she pushed the elevator's down button into its glowing ring.

"I'll call you when I get there," she said.

I smiled, managing some reserve. It was the nearest thing I'd heard from her that gave any indication she considered our being together something not wholly circumstantial. "There" was San Francisco, where she was to give a lecture. "When" would be tonight, the second Sunday in March.

The elevator doors closed, taking with her, it seemed, all the light and air in the hallway. I shut the door and leaned my full weight against it. I was physically exhausted — after all, we'd gotten precious little sleep all weekend — but mentally I was restless, hyper-alert. The room smelled like her in its every pore — her Fifth Avenue perfume, her suede blouse, her Italian leather shoes, her salty skin, her scalp . . . I stopped myself.

I still had two hours left before check-out; though she had left me with the key to turn in, the bill was all paid. I was grateful for the lag time. The room seemed to me ripe with secrets, as if — because she had spent so many recent hours here — she might have trailed clues, revealed herself in stray things left behind or small impressions made, artifacts too humble to study when she herself was present.

I investigated the bathroom first, flicked on its full arsenal of lights, the small, round bulbs around the mirror making it look like a movie star's dressing room. Nothing of hers here, and everything intact; the little plastic bottles of hotel shampoo and hand cream apparently did not interest her.

On the way out, I nearly missed it. There, on the peach marble sink, was a tissue imprinted with the outline of her lipsticked lips. I brought it close to my own lips; it was still fragrant. Hadn't I kissed this same lipstick off her lips these last two nights? Or had it already faded into our room-service sandwiches by then?

I carried the tissue carefully; it would either become a relic or just the first of many souvenirs. In any case, I knew my having it would offend her, would somehow open me up to her scorn. Because even then I suspected that displays of sentiment were, to her, dangerous and humiliating, what hearing a fireworks display was to a war veteran: an echo of some more powerful and frightening showdown with mortality.

I continued scanning. I was a detective at the scene of a crime, scouring the place for evidence that she had been here, and that I had been here with her. Because already the reality of it seemed to be seeping out of the room, evaporating like dew in the light of the maturing morning. I had to stay forever, I thought with faint panic, because to leave meant to return to cope with all the chaos my being here had created, and for what? For what exactly?

From the window I could see most of Central Park, looking, from this vantage of thirty-two stories, like some lush and untamed prairie. Every few minutes, a plane pointed its nose up into the clouds and vanished silently into the light blue haze. I knew there was no way she could have gotten to Kennedy Airport already, but still I let myself imagine that she was on each plane, so that I could play out again and again the sweet torture of her leaving. Was she peering out the window for a parting glimpse of New York, wondering whether she could pick out the general vicinity of the hotel, wondering whether I was still here, in our dewy, secret-filled room? Or was she already asleep (asleep the way I knew now she slept, neatly and tightly curled) or involved in a lapful of work or coolly fending off the chatter of

some intrusive seatmate? Wherever she was, it wasn't
with me, and she had left me alone to cope with her
being here, and then being gone.

It's the nature of youth that you can't know its
power while it's upon you. I was no exception. Or
maybe I'm only saying that now because I'm just on
the other side of thirty, and when I spent that first
weekend with her, I was just on the other side of
twenty. What I mean is, maybe I've reduced the
differences between us to the fact that we were
seventeen years apart, and maybe there were a
million other things that were just as important, a
million other things that could draw two people
together and pull them apart again.

I don't deny that I was attracted to her for being
older as much as she was to me for being younger.
And younger I was, enough to feel that there was
something intrinsically alluring and desirable about her
being thirty-nine.

Did I mention she was famous?

Now I don't mean famous in the sense of being a
household — say, my parents' household — word. You
could not walk into any supermarket or mall in
America, say her name and expect most people —
say, nine out of ten — not to draw a blank. But there
were other places you could go — certain college
towns, seaside resorts, gay bookstores, any gay
gathering, actually — and people, and I mean women,
mostly, would not only know her name but would
practically genuflect. It must have been a very odd

thing for her to be a gay goddess, a radical prophet
pinup in some circles, and then confront the larger
world and be despised or simply overlooked.

But if you were gay and a woman in any of the
last few decades, it was pretty much impossible *not*
to know her name. Since her surprise Off-Broadway
hit in the seventies, *Dykes and Other Strangers,* she
had made as much money talking about plays as she
did writing new ones. By the time I met her, there
was even something of a backlash. She had some
mileage on her by then, and though no one under
thirty can reasonably be expected to understand how
it happens, she had begun to mellow, to show
glimmers of the conciliatory, to prefer hibernation to
public displays of outage, to allow ghosts of past
regrets and disappointments to occasionally paralyze
her. But the place that she'd arrived at seemed to
me, at twenty-two, paved with nothing but romance
and glamor. What I had no way of knowing was that,
by thirty-nine, you could also accumulate an awful lot
of ghosts.

I'd like to think I would have done things
differently now than I did then, but I can't say
exactly how. And the truth is, I probably handled
things better then, propelled, as I was, by lust and
good will and a belief in people's basically decent
motives. Later I became too cautious and calculating,
and while I imagine that I might have been able to
beat her at her own game, I realize that these were
not even the terms then, that she would have sniffed
out a person like me today, the way a hypnotist can
sniff out a doubter who won't let herself go under.

* * * * *

I was, the very first time I met her, a cub
reporter at a downtown weekly newspaper called
Hip. "Alternative" was how it was described, as in an
alternative to the *New York Times*es of the world.
This was in the early eighties, when it was a
genuinely fresh impulse, and not a gimmick in
triplicate the way downtown papers have become.
The trouble was, the advertising world was not yet
ready for us, so we were constantly on the brink of
extinction. This added to the heady sense of
risk-taking on the part of the editorial staff.

No one on staff cared more than I did when Zena
Beth Frazer's latest collection of essays, *Hot Air*, was
published, timed for a Valentine's Day release. Its
deliberately irreverent title summed up her assessment
of popular culture and its generally homophobic
ways. Certainly a lesbian-feminist attack on
mainstream movies, theater and media was something
the editors knew they had to cover, but the veteran
reporters had more of a taste for scandals than
standard publicity-tour interviews. So it was
considered low priority and they felt benevolent
assigning it to me. And how could they have known
what it meant to me, that I had fantasized about
meeting her since I was thirteen? I agonized for days
over what to wear and then, deciding that nothing I
owned would do, spent money I could ill afford on a
new pair of cuffed slacks and a tuxedo blouse with
mother of pearl buttons.

I got to the interview early and paced myself
dizzy in the lobby of the hotel. It was evidently her
regular place when she was in town, one of the
grand dames along Central Park West, that strip of
elegant and hushed hotels that made up the single

most expensive piece of real estate in all of
Manhattan. The lobby's rug was slightly, almost
imperceptibly shabby, likely by design. Something
about it communicated tradition and old money, the
way few new things could.

Her room was the same way, I saw, when I was
finally summoned by the press rep. Nothing flashy or
trendy about it; it was almost austere. And there she
was, in complete relief in a red silk dress, with her
arched, highly mobile black eyebrows, her keen, light
brown eyes, her tight-lipped, mischievous smile. She
looked much the way she did in all the photos I had
seen and studied; sounded, when she greeted me and
ushered me in, much the way she had on all the
radio interviews I had heard, and yet all that left
something out. In person, her energy level was
palpable. She hummed with a kind of impatience; she
seemed restless for action. And yet she sat on the
edge of the bed almost demurely, nearly a picture of
a Southern society lady. That was her secret weapon,
why mainstream critics and theater people and
talk-show hosts loved to spotlight her even as she
delivered knockout punches to their pride. To look at
her, you would not have thought this was the same
woman who once suggested that male politicians
have their penises strapped down for the duration of
their office, to force them to think less primitively
and more rationally.

The press rep, a blonde in a wool suit, stayed in
the room with us, and I was secretly grateful.
Otherwise, the sheer strain of the circumstances —
Zena Beth Frazer and I alone in a hotel room with
nothing but a king-size bed between us — simply
would have been too much.

I fussed only briefly with my tape recorder, eager
to speak before the tremble in my wrists spread.
"You say in one of your essays that you want to
keep talking about being gay until there's no reason
to talk about it anymore," I said, hearing my voice
come out thin, reluctant, quavery. "Is it fair to say
that that's been the main mission of your whole
career?"

She didn't waste much time throwing the question
back in my face; that was her trademark. "I don't
know if you're gay or not," she said, locking eyes
with me for just a moment before casting what
seemed to be an indifferent glance out the window,
"but no one will feel safe coming out until it's not
an insult, not a threat to safety and security to be
called gay, until someone straight could be called gay
without that being just a mistake instead of an
indictment. That should be all our missions." She
turned back to me, pausing for emphasis the way a
trial lawyer might upon producing the murder
weapon.

My throat tightened as I listened to the tape
recorder quietly whirring nearby. It was an expression
she was fond of, that "I don't know if you're gay or
not," a debating tool, perfectly politically correct:
don't dare assume anyone's straight. Still I half
wondered if she expected me to answer, anyway.
That was another asset — the propaganda always
sounded intimate, personal.

In the few seconds that she waited, a lifetime of
erotic possibilities occurred to me. I was young, and
I believed that everyone had a point of entry,
everyone was theoretically available, even the rich

and famous. What I didn't know then was that this was *especially* true for the rich and famous, at least those who were gay, because they were isolated and conspicuous all at once, limited in avenues of meeting lovers, except for those few who were trapped in the same fishbowl. But I didn't know that then. All I had was an arrogance born of optimism. I didn't know yet that as people got older they sometimes lost their nerve, they got scared, they got comfortable, they occasionally even got God.

"You came of age in the movement when it was just separating from mainstream feminist groups. Looking back, do you regret that? Do you wish straight feminists had been forced to take on the fight for lesbian rights, in the interest of strength in numbers?"

"Well, for one thing," she said, smiling slowly and drawing out her words as if she were relaxing after a good meal, "too much regret will send you to an early grave and I don't recommend it. So no, I don't regret it. And lesbians have certainly taken on feminist concerns, so I think we're all carrying the ball in the same direction. Straight women and lesbians have a lot more in common than either side is happy to admit. We all care about the environment and day care and not blowing the planet to bits in some fireworks display of testosterone. But straight women have to get into bed at night with men, and that's bound to make them feel a little more inclined to compromise."

I knew I was getting great quotes, and began moving through my list of questions smoothly; the quake in my voice was beginning to subside. "What do you say to critics who charge that it's a shame gay writers and artists waste their talent writing only about gay subjects?"

I saw her eyes widen in alarm. "I've heard that all my life. 'Why don't you write for the big leagues — you could make much more money, get much more attention.' But that's so hostile and homophobic on so many levels. Hetero is better, is one assumption. Or that you can change your internal inspiration just like you can change shoes. Would they ever dream of telling a black writer to write about more important concerns — like the white community? No, but they can still say it to us. And our answer has to be that we won't stop, that we will continue to claim our voices and our territory and our issues."

The outer edges of nervousness had nearly numbed when the press rep, who had remained respectfully silent the whole half hour, stood and stretched, ever so daintily, indicating that the interview was over.

"Well, it was a pleasure," Zena Beth Frazer said. "You asked thoughtful questions. I don't always expect that."

My mouth went cottony and the strength seemed to sap from my legs; the combination of the compliment and the fact that our meeting was over was too much to take in all at once. Whatever composure I had been able to maintain during the interview vanished as I stood up, trying to assemble my equipment. A faint tremble vibrated in my ribcage.

"Well, let me ask you one last question, then," I blurted. "Are you free for dinner tonight?"

As soon as it was out, I felt my cheeks on fire

with embarrassment. How horrible and awkward; of course she would have to refuse.

"Oh —" she said, "that's so sweet, but they —" She gestured over her shoulder at the press rep, "— have me booked every waking moment, and even some non-waking moments." The rep and I laughed appreciatively, sympathetically.

I nearly believed her. When she shut the door after me, I charged for the elevator and escape, made a wrong turn, and collided squarely with a paisley print wall.

It was mid-March, nearly a month later, before I heard from her again. Of course, there was no reason to expect to hear from her at all, ever, and I even managed to forget about her for days at a time. I had sent her the story as soon as it was out. It was flattering and funny and made us both look good, I thought. But only her publisher had sent an acknowledging letter.

I was at the far end of the room, digging through some reference books for an article I was working on about bribery in the department of traffic violations, when the receptionist shouted for me. "Ecco — your line! Zena Beth Frazer."

It was the habit of the receptionist's to shout out callers' names. This way, reporters knew how quickly they wanted to sprint across the floor for their calls. We were all used to hearing the names of the revered and the despised shouted in the receptionist's slightly nasal voice, and only a few names created any kind of pause or stir. A member of the Weather

Underground who'd been a fugitive for fifteen years
was always good for impact, but otherwise, we were
a tough crowd.

So I wouldn't say a hush exactly fell over the
newsroom but it quieted down enough for me to
hear my own sneakers squeak across the floor, and to
notice a few people abruptly hang up their own
phones. It wasn't the fact that Zena Beth Frazer was
calling, as much as she was calling *me,* an as yet
undistinguished cub reporter. It was nothing to have
gotten the interview in the first place, given the
paper's reputation and the fact that she had a new
book out, but to have an unsolicited call from her,
perhaps social, upset a few veterans' sense of
protocol. But all this barely registered with me. I was
too busy scouring my mind for something to say as
an opener that was both charming and highly
charged with sexual innuendo.

"Hello?" I said.

"Joyce? It's Zena Beth Frazer." Her slight Southern
lilt was more appealingly apparent over the phone.
What's more, the sound of our first names so casually
posed in one sentence, *her* sentence, raised
goosebumps up and down my arms.

"Yes, so I heard, and, thanks to our special
paging system, so did the entire newsroom."

"Ah — are you embarrassed?"

"Not at all. Flattered. I just don't want to
disappoint them." On the phone, I found, I could
take chances. I had to: who knew how many other
chances there would be?

She laughed, a lighthearted, summery sound. I
pulled a chair under me in self-defense. "Well, maybe
you won't have to," she said. "I wanted to know if I

could have a rain check on that offer you made back
when you interviewed me. I'm going to be in New
York tomorrow night — I have to fly out to San
Francisco on Sunday — and we Southerners hate to
be rude and turn down a dinner invitation, especially
when it comes from someone so attractive."

I had never really understood the term "hot flash"
until that moment. The blush spread over my face
and neck like a brush fire and robbed me of
intelligible speech. I managed enough, however, to
arrange to meet her at the same hotel as the last
time at seven the following night.

When we hung up, I pulled a pad over and
pretended to be absorbed by whatever was written
there; unfortunately, it was the dance review
department's lunch order so it wasn't all that
distracting. I didn't trust myself to walk across the
room and out the front door where I could charge
around the block hooting my victory at the skyline.
Instead, I sat there, letting the triumph cool into
reality. Then I thought of two things: if she had
really been hoping to see me, why had she waited
until the day before to call? And what in the world
was I going to tell Elaine?

I met Elaine the way you are not supposed to
meet women in New York whom you eventually
grow to care about: at a bar. It was at one of those
firetraps that were common in the early eighties, one
that had stayed open for barely a few weeks. How
we managed to be there on the same night at the
same hour and make eye contact in that

smoke-choked, nightmare-lit bar, I'll never know. But
we did.

I coveted her immediately. She was tall, nearly my
height, and full-bodied to my lean; long, dark, wavy
hair framed her face. I had gotten very good, after
years of trying to fall in love in bars, at sizing up a
woman with just a look. An astute, peripheral glance
and I could tell the airheads from the snobs, the
bores from the druggies, in the time it took to ask,
"Do you want to dance?" And what I saw in Elaine's
face was compassion, sincerity, generosity — things I
had learned the hard way never to take for granted
in New York.

But we discovered that we had something more
than that early attraction; we had a common
background, a similar point of reference. She had also
been raised Catholic and had grown up in a borough
of New York City — Brooklyn. And though she
earned a living as a computer programmer, her first
love, and her dream, was to be a photographer.

What surprised me was that, even after a year of
our seeing each other and feeling us grow closer in
surprising spurts (like wading into a stream and losing
your footing and realizing it had opened up into an
ocean), loving her did not cancel out the wild
longings I felt toward the occasional other woman.
For weeks on end I would be so happy with our life
together but then I would fall into conversation at a
party with a woman whose face or hands or voice
would haunt me for days. The feeling always passed,
like a fit or a bad cold, and I would return fully to
Elaine, vaguely remorseful and distinctly grateful that I
had not blown it.

But Zena Beth Frazer I was completely powerless

to resist. I knew that from the second I met her. The struggle I engaged in was mostly for conscience's sake.

I had known about Zena Beth since I was a teenager, from the time I had my first stirring that I might love women. She had soon become a fixture, a constant, a fact of life.

She was, when I first became aware of her, just at the crest of her popularity, making the gossip columns with her new lover, a world champion skier with a nouveau fortune and androgynous good looks. I used to spend hours poring over the news photos with their cryptic captions which the sophisticated were always able to decipher (*Zena Beth Frazer making tracks on the Aspen slopes with Helena Zoë*). It always struck me that it was Zena Beth, the non-professional skier, who would have a protective grip somewhere on Helena's body — her elbow or shoulder. I used to fantasize about running into the two of them in a Greenwich Village cafe, offering to buy them cappucinos, and chatting for hours about life imitating athletics.

What is there to say about the fascination? I know that at the time I could not really have explained it, though I would have told anyone who asked that I thought Zena Beth witty, courageous and irreverent, a bold writer and thinker, and not least of all, very hot (and most of those things were true). But at twenty-two, I had no way of knowing that that was just the bait. The real lure, I think now, is that I saw her as my rendezvous with immortality; in some subterranean way I believed that if I breathed the same rarified air as she did, if I rubbed against the secret elixir of her skin, then I would be somehow

more worthy, more worthwhile, myself. In some ways
I did not fully exist yet in my own imagination
(because what else do we do in living our lives but
imagine ourselves into being?) and she gave me some
very interesting ideas.

"I'm having dinner with Nikki tomorrow night
and staying over at her place," I lied to Elaine over
the phone.

"Oh, that should be nice," she said, without a
trace of suspicion.

And why not? I had never given her reason to
suspect me of anything before. And there was
nothing unusual about my seeing Nikki alone: Nikki
was my best friend, a compadre from college days,
before Elaine supplanted her in every way. Still, there
were subjects on which Nikki knew me better than
anyone.

"So what's new with her, anyway?" Elaine asked.

It was unbearable to me, having to play out the
lie. "Well, she tried to sound nonchalant about it, but
I think she's falling in love with some straight woman
at work."

This was true; I was not, at least, making this
part up. I had talked to Nikki long enough to ask her
to cover for me if Elaine happened to call or ask
about "our evening" later.

"A straight woman?" Elaine asked. "Does the
woman know?"

Does she know? This was the endless refrain of
all our secret-infested lives. The password, the club

key, necessary before unlocking some approximation
of the truth.

"Well, no — I mean, I don't think she's told her
yet. I think that's what she wants to talk to me
about. To get my opinion. What do you think?"

I knew it was a mistake the second it was out of
my mouth.

"What do I think? I don't even have to think.
How could you keep something so important from
someone you call a friend?"

Elaine sounded faintly disgusted, as if I were a
heathen guest at a holy feast who had just said
something blasphemous. Why was she playing this
awful game of roulette with me? If she knew my
story was totally bogus, why didn't she just call me
to the mat on it? "I'll miss you," she said, going
warm and fuzzy.

"It'll be the first Friday night in a long time that I
won't have you in my bed."

I pictured us, legs intertwined, her long, dark hair
across my pillow and hers, the way we would be
before drifting off to sleep together, and was seized
by a sudden spasm of regret and longing. "Well, you
could join us, or I'll take the train back into
Brooklyn. . . ." I was reckless, out of control.

"No, no, you two have your girls' night out."

It was the sort of kind, selfless gesture Elaine was
so often capable of. For one feverish moment, I
nearly called the whole thing off. Why was I so eager
to spend an evening with a distant stranger, someone
probably egotistical, pretentious and judgmental, when
I had Elaine who knew and loved me so well and so
long?

"I love you," Elaine said, as she was hanging up.
"I love you, too," I said, completely hating
myself.

— 2 —

When I got to the lobby of Zena Beth's hotel, I was mildly surprised to find it looking exactly the way I had remembered it from a month before when I had been here as her interviewer. It struck me as inconsistent somehow, since now the world had changed. A month ago, I had been a mere cub reporter at *Hip,* an insignificant blip. Now I felt as though I had been chosen, earmarked, set aside.

I dialed her room number from the lobby phone. "Zena Beth?" I asked when a Southern voice said hello. "It's Joyce. I'm downstairs."

19

"Oh, come on up."

In the elevator, I studied the bouquet of six coral roses I had brought. I pressed my face into their soft fragrant petals and inhaled, hoping the scent would steady me. But my stomach bucked like a dinghy in a tropical storm.

When I stepped off the elevator, Zena Beth was standing in the doorway of the room, holding the door open. In snugly fitting black pants and a jade blouse, she looked a notch more butch than she had the day I saw her in her red silk dress and heels. She smiled as she spotted the flowers. "A woman after my own heart," she said.

She closed the door behind us and I shrugged out of my coat, trying to seem brisk and unassuming, as if we were here for just another interview. The room was softly lit with one glowing lamp on the dresser, the bathroom lights were on as if after her recent use, and there was the conspicuous absence of any publisher's representative.

Suddenly I had no words. I was an impostor, clearly in over my head, and I fought the urge to bolt in terror. Who was I to think I could be any kind of entertaining companion to Zena Beth Frazer on a Friday night in Manhattan? I shoved my hands into the pockets of my freshly dry cleaned tuxedo pants and felt my upper lip grow clammy.

"So how was work today? What's happening at *Hip?*" she called from the bathroom, where I heard her unwrapping the crinkly paper from the flowers. "You know," she said, emerging and heading for the phone, "those bathroom glasses just aren't going to do for these roses. Thank you again — they're just so beautiful. We Southerners, you know, just love our

flowers." I watched her back as she dialed. "Yes,
Fred, good evening. I believe I'm going to need a
vase for some flowers I've just received." She
pronounced "vase" with a short "a."

When she turned around, she seemed unnerved to
find me watching her. She gave me a tight smile
before going back into the bathroom to take up her
monologue again. "I thought we'd go over to the
Paris theater and catch the Truffaut movie. It starts at
eight-twenty. Do you like Truffaut?"

I had never seen a Truffaut movie in my life —
though I had been in the Paris theater, which was, at
least, something. I began to do a rapid-fire mental
inventory of all the things she'd have been likely to
have done or seen or known that I hadn't or didn't
or couldn't, and I began to feel a little lightheaded.
Before I had a chance to answer her, there was a
knock at the door. "I'll get it," I called, happy for
the chance to be purposeful.

A young bellhop was cradling a crystal vase in
both hands. Suddenly, Zena Beth was at my elbow,
relieving him of it. "Oh, thank you," she said,
pressing a bill into his hand. "I'll put them in water
myself."

She shut the door on his grateful face and for a
moment we were side by side in the narrow foyer. I
could smell the suede of her blouse, mixed with
some intoxicating perfume that, I could have sworn,
simply bypassed my nose and entered my
bloodstream directly.

"Perfect," she said to the vase and headed into
the bathroom again.

The fact that I had remained standing after having
been in such close proximity to her made me more

bold. I leaned into the peach-marble bathroom to watch her carefully arranging the flowers in water.

"So the Truffaut is okay with you?" she asked.

"Great," I said. It struck me all at once that she was nervous, too, filling up the room with her directives and questions to smother the silence, which, in this setting, was palpably intimate.

She looked up, one rose frozen between her fingers. "You have quite an intense stare," she said, just a dash defensive.

And a lot, I suspected, rattled. This I could handle: Zena Beth off-balance. "It's just that it's a lot to take in," I said, gesturing to include her and the hotel room all at once.

She smiled slowly to acknowledge the compliment. "You're sure you're not just a little bit Southern?" she said, equilibrium regained, and her attention back on the roses. She stepped back, satisfied, finally, with their arrangement.

I moved aside so she could carry the brimming vase into the room. She put it on the night table next to the bed. "Well, we should start walking over," she said, pushing back a loose suede sleeve to reveal a Rolex. "I thought we could grab a bite after the movie."

"Sounds good," I said, relieved, actually, because I couldn't have eaten just then if my life had depended on it. I picked up my coat from the foot of the bed where I'd tossed it. "This is your favorite hotel in the city, I take it?"

"Absolutely," she said. "Small, quiet, private."

I pushed aside the light green curtain to investigate the view. Part of Central Park West glittered underneath us, and the old-fashioned street

lamps glowed like halos in the cold air. *Privacy,* I
considered. Such an understated reference to the vast
difference in the way we lived. I never had to worry
about wily photographers snapping pictures of me
and the woman I might be sleeping with, never had
to worry that any public statement I made might end
up on the newswires.

I let the curtain go and walked over to run my
finger along the dark wood desk. There was some
writing paper out and a Montblanc pen across it, fat
as a cigar. Who, I wondered, was getting a note
dashed off from her as she hopped between cities? A
far-off quiver of jealousy rippled through me.

Zena Beth was in front of the closet, snapping a
leather jacket closed around her. It was deep maroon,
almost black, with dolman sleeves, a cinched waist
and padded shoulders. "What a spectacular jacket," I
said, feeling suddenly provincial in my modest
herringbone overcoat.

"Oh, thank you," she said, sounding embarrassed.
"I don't get to wear it much back home. People look
at me oddly. Not that that's anything new."

We both laughed. She didn't have to tell me that
home for her was Mountville, a little town at the
foot of the Smoky Mountains in North Carolina. She
wrote lovingly about the place often, as if it were a
kind of mecca or best friend.

We walked down the hallway to the elevator. For
a fleeting moment I felt that we were old lovers,
companionable in our silence, comfortable in our
familiar rhythms with each other. Eyes fixed on the
descending numbers, she said, "How did you happen
to know that coral is my favorite color rose?"

"I didn't," I said, startled into frankness. "I

happen to like them a lot, myself — and, besides,
lavender seemed too obvious."

She smiled, a sadder smile than I'd seen so far.
How curious and cautious, I thought, that she had
held on to this observation about the roses so long
after I handed them over.

When we stepped onto the street, the March air
hit us full in the face, and she seemed to shrink
inside her jacket, like a turtle into her shell. "I'm
basically a hothouse plant out of the hothouse when
I come up north. I don't know how you Yankees
take it."

We moved into the rushing New York crowd and
headed in the direction of the theater. It was only a
few blocks away, across from the Plaza, the kind of
immense, gilded hotel that, I was sure now, she
hated. Several black stretch limos would be lined up
in front of its carpeted outdoor steps, and bellhops in
red jackets with gold-capped shoulders would be
helping women in furs and spindly heels into them.
When I saw her shiver, I summoned my nerve and
slipped my arm through hers.

"Oh, you don't mind?" she asked. I looked at her
blankly. "I mean, not everyone wants to be seen on
the street with me on her arm."

"What I want," I said, shaking off this latest
reference to her public life, "is for you not to freeze
to death on me before we've even seen the movie."

We walked the last block in silence. I was
concentrating on navigating the sidewalk without
tripping or bumping into another couple, or without
jostling her arm too much. I was also marveling at
the fact that she was shorter than I was by several
inches, something I'd managed not to notice before.

There was only a short line for the movie and Zena Beth got to the window first, paying for the two tickets. "Thank you," I said quickly, deciding it would be tacky to offer to pay for just mine, and absurd to offer belatedly to pay for both. Still, I hated the idea that she might think I *expected* her to pay because everyone knew she was a woman of considerable means.

We had our pick of seats, and I was nearly giddy. Here I was, about to do something as ordinary as watch a movie with Zena Beth Frazer. "I like to catch these kinds of films when I'm up here," she said. "Back home, we have to wait a little longer — and some don't get to us at all."

The lights went down shortly and the movie started. It was some black and white affair, a murder mystery whose tone was somewhere between Hitchcock and the Marx Brothers. I had no idea how to take it or what, particularly, was going on.

Zena Beth, however, seemed to be absorbed. And I was prepared to defer to her opinion, even if it was that the film was more remarkable than the Second Coming of Christ. Perhaps I was just not applying myself properly, being distracted by the scent of Zena Beth so close to me in the darkness.

By the time the lights came back up, it was almost ten o'clock. Zena Beth looked refreshed, even wakeful in the semi-dingy glow of the theater. "Ready? Or do you want to see it again?" she asked, all fourth-grade school-yard tease.

"Well, normally I would, but in this case I think it would ruin the effect. I might actually understand it."

She laughed, and the sound made me lightheaded

with happiness. "Also, I'll bet you're starved. God knows I am."

As we emerged from the cocoon of warmth and darkness, the night air seemed sharp-edged and layered with iciness. Zena Beth hunched her shoulders forward miserably. "Would you mind if we just ate in the room?" she said, looking nearly fearful that, presumably, I might object and want to travel in the cold to a restaurant. For my part, I was thrilled that I was still part of her evening plans. Up to this point, it wouldn't have surprised me if she said goodnight at the hotel's revolving door.

"Some people don't mind the cold," she went on, moving too briskly for me to offer any kind of warming grip. "I have an ex-lover who's absolutely impervious to it. I guess when you ski, you have to be. I'd be out there on the slopes with her while she practiced, feeling my eyelashes freezing together, and she'd be frolicking like a Dalmatian on the beach. I used to tell her she must boil her blood in the morning."

I managed a laugh but I was concentrating on keeping my balance. Even though I knew as sure as the sky was blue that Zena Beth Frazer loved women, there was something nearly exhilarating about hearing the small details confirmed from her own lips. As though that wasn't enough, here she was, referring casually to Helena Zoë as if she were the girl next door or someone she'd picked up at the K-Mart, instead of one of the most famous sport faces in the modern world. But it also irked me that I couldn't tell what her real point was. Did she believe that I really might not know to whom she was referring? Or was she just innocently complaining about the weather? Or did she mean it to signal something else entirely, namely, the issue of her high-profile love life or the superiority of that affair? Seeing her sheer misery now in the relatively mild mid-twenties of a New York March, it was hard, nearly impossible, to imagine her on bare mountainsides, exposed to whipping wind and lashing snow. In fact, it seemed so out of character that it troubled me vaguely that she had done it. It hinted at a kind of self-sacrifice that could only be unhealthy, a kind I hoped I never would feel.

Everyone knew that Helena Zoë had been the one to leave Zena Beth Frazer — and to do it for a closeted female news anchor — so I did not think it wise to pursue that possible conversational avenue. But before I had a chance to change the subject, Zena Beth returned to it.

"She finally moved out to Colorado to be near the skiing but she really prefers Switzerland. Now that's my idea of a nightmare locale."

I was totally at a loss, so I merely smiled into the gusty night air. Was she to have me believe that an irreconcilable difference over *climate* was the reason they broke up?

"Nothing would get you to leave North Carolina, I bet," I said. It seemed a safe remark; "nothing" could mean the weather, if she felt like being coy, or it could stand for "not even Helena Zoë" if she felt like being frank.

"It's hard. Not everyone falls in love with the place like I did. So it means I'm usually on a plane every time I want some female companionship. Mountville is not known for its large population of attractive dykes." She laughed, at what particular private memory, I didn't know. But it struck me as possible that she might have had more than one night of sex she regretted. "And since I'm on a plane so much for my work, too, I figure I'm in the air more than I'm on the ground."

"Well, I'm glad you're on the ground now," I said, as we pushed through the revolving doors of the hotel.

"You keep making comments like that, darlin', and my head's gonna get so big I won't stay on the ground for long."

For a moment I felt the thrill of our new sparring, but I couldn't completely shake the feeling that she was mostly grading my approach rather than actually absorbing the sentiment.

She had left the lights on, so the room was still lit when we opened the door. She picked up the room service menu before she was even out of her coat. "I think I'll just do a turkey club," she said, handing me the menu and taking my coat to hang up. I surveyed the food options, weighing each for their potential humiliation factor — which ones would slide or snake or spill on me while we ate.

"A pair of turkeys sounds good to me," I said.

"As it must have to most of America when they elected our men in the White House."

I laughed as she gave our order. She sat on the bed, and, toe to heel, pushed off her black leather loafers. Not wanting to seem too familiar, I pulled the chair away from the desk and sat down there.

"So," she said, "you like living up here, despite the cold and the obscene cost of living?"

"It has its advantages. Besides, it's kind of an occupational hazard, being born here. Once you grow

up in New York, every other place seems too slow
or too dull or too simple. But I want to travel more,
see more of the country." I added this last hastily,
not wanting to discourage her if she was ever to
suggest I visit her in the Smoky Mountains. We'd
barely spent three hours together, and already I felt
myself planning outings for us for weeks and months
to come.

Such thoughts were as inappropriate as raucous
children in an elegant restaurant, but most women,
straight or gay, have trouble keeping them in check.
When women see threads, they tend to imagine
textures. Put two women together across a romantic
divide, and that texture quickly becomes an
auditorium-sized quilt. Not that this was all good, of
course. I'd seen the downside: for two women new
to an affair, the pull of sudden intimacy could be as
seductive — and dangerous — as quicksand.

But I sensed that Zena Beth policed herself
fiercely against such brushfires of passion, that she
kept the essential center of herself separate and apart.
I had no such defense.

Just then there was a knock at the door, and a
muffled voice called out, "Room service."

"I'll get it," she said, springing up. The same
bellhop as earlier wheeled in an elegant table set
with a white linen tablecloth, china and silverware.
Two silver domes were sitting atop each plate; he
lifted them with a flourish to reveal our hefty
sandwiches. "Terrific," she said, walking him to the
door. "Thank you," I heard him say as he was
stepping into the hallway.

I kept my desk chair, and Zena Beth pulled one
from the corner of the room and settled down to eat.

"I didn't realize how hungry I was till I laid eyes on a meal," she said.

We took turns swapping pieces of our history. I told her about growing up an only child in Queens, taking subways to school, being taught by nuns, hiding my romances from my parents, who were so thrilled to have a daughter who graduated college that they didn't hassle me about having my own apartment and no plans to get married. She told me about growing up on a farm with six brothers, coming to the big city, colliding with incredible good luck in the theater, and then returning to the countryside that spawned her. Not that this story was new to me. Anyone who had read even a few reviews of her work would know as much. I tried to get her to offer something beyond this stock bio, but nothing was forthcoming. She seemed to want to ask the questions, rather than answer them.

"So you're not out to your co-workers or parents?" she asked.

I took a swig of soda to buy some time. "Well, my general rule is that I don't lie to anyone — no made-up boyfriends or switched pronouns — but I don't necessarily feel compelled to tell the whole truth to everyone within shouting distance."

"It's got to be a burden, a kind of prison," she said, taking her napkin off her lap and laying it next to her nearly cleaned plate. I had barely nibbled the edge of my sandwich. I saw her glance at it, but she made no comment.

"No, I don't feel that way. The people who need to know get the message loud and clear." I smiled lasciviously, and she laughed.

"Let's make some room," she said casually.

Room for what, I wondered, feeling a little clammy as she wheeled the table out into the hallway. When she came back in, she lay diagonally across the bed on her side, her head propped up with one hand.

"Come talk to me some more," she said, patting the place next to her.

I sat cross-legged at the head of the bed, making a monstrous effort at nonchalance, too terrified to wonder what she might be up to. "Don't get me wrong," I said. "I'd like to see a time when everyone in the world who's gay would come out on the same day. Then everyone would see how many of us there are."

"Yes, that would be easy, wouldn't it?" I caught the mild reproach. "I used to think like that," she went on. "I thought people ought to make up their minds once and for all about something as important as whether to be out or not. Because that's the way I did it. But I didn't see till later that most people spend their whole lives struggling with it, making exceptions, going in and out of the closet."

She pulled off her watch and laid it on the night table. "A few of my lovers have been married women. That was when I was younger — now I don't like to double deal someone — and a few of them left their husbands. Not necessarily for me, I hasten to point out." She laughed. "But even when the women didn't remarry, and the whole of the world pitied them, I could see they weren't the ones really suffering. The men were. Women's energy is a special thing, and both men and women need it. Just look at married women — they have to have their women friends. But the men, they're all set. And when they lose a wife, they're mighty quick to replace her. It isn't sex drive, the way people say. It's women's energy and spirit that's just too hard for anyone to live without. That's why I think most women aren't shocked when they hear you're a lesbian. Even if they can't admit it, on the deepest level, they know *exactly* what you're talking about."

"Yes, gay until proven straight."

"Well, maybe that's too optimistic, even for me." She stretched delicately. "I don't know about you, but I'm getting kind of tired. You're welcome to stay here if you don't want to make the train trip all the way back to Queens."

My stomach crimped in fear. What was she proposing, exactly? A platonic sleepover? Wasn't she even going to try to kiss me? Or was this her idea of a proposition, the best she could do in the way of seduction?

"Of course, I can't promise I'll do anything . . ." she said, smiling slowly.

Oh, so this was clarification. "I'll take my chances."

"I thought you might."

I blushed hotly. "Um, actually, do you have anything I could throw on, something to sleep in?" I mustered up the nerve to ask only because my two other choices — coming back out fully dressed or buck naked — were equally absurd.

"Oh —" she said, getting up to fold open the closet door. She held out a red T-shirt. "It's my favorite color."

"I'll try to do it justice."

Behind the closed door of the bathroom, I

allowed myself a moment of panic. I hadn't brought an overnight bag — that would have seemed too presumptuous. But I had tucked some essentials — makeup, toothbrush — into a small pouch I had carried for this express purpose. And I had left a change of clothes in the closet at the office, which was, mercifully, nearby.

She had left things sufficiently open-ended, I felt, so that if sleep did suddenly overcome her, I had no right to feel misled. Actually, that option was beginning to have more and more appeal. What did I know about making love to Zena Beth Frazer? And besides, I felt a bit taken for granted. Was I supposed to slip into the phone booth and burst back out as Supervixen? Where were all the steamy kisses, the half-undressed gropings, that one took for some sign of interest?

At the moment, there was nothing to be done but to get into the T-shirt and get out of the bathroom. But when I pulled it over my head, I realized my dilemma. It was a good two sizes too small for me, and constricted like an Ace bandage. My breasts were plastered to my chest; actually, they were nearly squeezed into my armpits. I tried to tug it loose without stretching it hopelessly out of shape. To my horror, it stopped short just below my navel, so I kept my bikini underwear on. Then I took a deep breath and opened the bathroom door.

Zena Beth had turned off the overhead light, leaving the whole room lit only by the modest glow of the bedside lamp. She was under the covers, on her stomach, her arms folded under her head.

"Shirt's a little small," I mumbled, as I lifted the

covers and slid into bed next to her. And there was
no mistaking what I quickly saw: she was completely
naked.

"Take it off, then," she said, leaning over and
helping me wrestle out of the shirt, which she let fall
to the floor. She lingered over me, casually resting
her own small breasts against mine. I tried to keep
myself from going rigid with fear.

"It was very sweet of you to bring the roses,"
she said, a look of childlike joy on her face. "I can't
tell you how long it's been since someone's
pampered me."

I reached up and gingerly ran the tips of my
fingers through her hair, which was baby fine and,
when I pushed it back, brushed lightly with gray. "I
find that hard to believe," I whispered.

"No, it's true. And it's been a long time since I've
been to bed with a woman. I'm afraid I'll be
terrible."

"Shhhh, it's okay," I said, letting my other hand
trail down her gently sloped back. Even then, I
wondered if it was a tactic: make your younger lover
feel confident by pretending that you're the one
who's nervous. But it worked; I felt ferociously
tender.

She lowered her lips to mine and we kissed
tentatively, just a grazing of lips and tongues. "Let me
get this light — it's in my eyes," she said, plunging
us into almost total darkness.

"Wait, can't we open up those curtains?" I asked.
"I'd like to be able to see you."

She jumped up quickly, a certain edge to her
movements, as if she were a spring coiled a little too
tightly, and reeled back the curtains. The room

glowed with the strange gray light of a New York evening. She stood there for a moment looking out, as straight and unwavering as a tree, as narrow and unself-conscious as an adolescent boy caught unaware at a river's edge. There was nothing especially feminine about her streamlined silhouette, and it was hard to suppress a fleeting comparison to Elaine. And yet, I felt an almost primal need to touch her, to cover her body with my own and claim her, the way that I imagined sheer sexual power could claim.

She returned to bed, and this time I didn't let her retreat under the sheets. I scanned her body with my hands and lips, delighted to find her nipples large and dark and meaty. The strong muscles of her arms and legs lurked like rocks below the surface of her skin, which was slightly soft with sun and years, as if it might tear if I prodded it too suddenly. Her hands were not what I expected — the creamed and sheltered hands of a wealthy playwright — but weathered and nicked instead like a laborer's. I imagined them on horses' reins and saddles, hauling and lifting and hammering, the way a woman alone on a farm would have to. Her hands seemed to me, at that moment in the half-light, more forthcoming than her face, more willing to reveal her secrets, and I turned them over and kissed the palms, and over again to press the knuckles against my cheeks.

"I knew you'd have beautiful breasts," she breathed, cupping them as I leaned over her, and that touch was more than I needed to be pushed over the edge. All self-consciousness and hesitancy evaporated in the flame of passion.

She whimpered and moaned under my touch, making me lightheaded with glee. I'd never been

with a woman who was so vocal; all trace of her
daytime reticence was abandoned. When I finally
pressed my lips between her legs, finding her sweet
and warm and finely tuned, we were both damp and
loud with pleasure, me nearly hoarse with my own
shallow breathing, she groaning softly for more,
urging my fingers faster and deeper inside her, until
she gripped my back hard and cried out.

She left herself not a beat for recovery. She rolled
me over and in seconds I felt her complete authority.
It was as if she had known my body for years, or,
more than that, as if my body hadn't known itself till
she found it. The advantage of her strength became
clear: she was tireless and powerful, her fingers
expert and merciless, till I thought the top of my
head would simply lift off, and my toes curl into
themselves. Her lips were everywhere at once. I felt
that I was in a lashing storm, my body raked and
exposed, not my own at all. She opened me up and
devoured me all at once, and whispered things that
shocked and gratified. I felt myself dropping from
some high and dangerous place, and then, exhausted
and helpless, I gave in to her lips, which found the
place again, drawing fire from inside till I was
swollen and fevered, tied by a lifeline to the pulse of
her mouth, racing across a finish line, desperate for
release.

"Tell me how to make you come again," she
breathed against my earlobe, not waiting for my
answer, not really. Instead, she pulled me on top of
her, so that I straddled her, and she thrust her hips
against me. "You're so wet," she murmured into my
neck. "It makes me crazy." I felt the whole world's
pull of gravity at my groin again, and cried out with

my arms around her head. She dropped me down on my back and pinned me, gripping my thigh between both of hers, and grinding in long strokes till she shuddered and finally came to rest.

We cooled down slowly, all curled and sealed to each other, sticky and steamy and sweet-smelling. I traced the outline of her cheek and neck and shoulder; she tangled her hands wordlessly in my hair. We were silent, in fact, quiet as people in holy places, reverent, humbled, awed. But in my head, words rattled to break free, words like love and need, words that, I realized, despite all this, were far too risky and raw. I felt naked without them now, and thought of Elaine again; "I love you" was a kind of seal, a chant we used, that made our sex a sacrament.

I had lost all track of time, except that my body felt the kind of pleasured numbness I'd known only after hours of lovemaking. Zena Beth twitched once in my arms as she tripped into some dream. I lay there a long while, breathing in the scent of her scalp, straining in the dim light to admire her body. When I tried to roll over, she whimpered a little and clamped her arm tightly around me from behind. What a whole different language she spoke in her sleep, I marveled, and would it make any difference at all in the morning?

− 3 −

She stirred first. I opened my eyes and realized we had fallen asleep with the curtains wide open; sun flooded the room, but we had still managed to sleep through the earliest light. I tried to persuade her with a hug to stay in bed, but she struggled slightly; I suspected that to insist would have been dangerous, like trying to pin a butterfly by its wings.

She sprang to her feet, stretching her arms high over her head and swinging down into a deep toe-touch. "I'm having lunch with old friends," she said, tugging the curtains shut a bit. I pulled the covers up under my chin to fight off the chill left by her retreating warmth. "Then I have a radio interview. It's a debate, I think. One of the theater producers I skewer in the book."

"Ah," I said, trying to muster enthusiasm. I was a little less interested in her mind now than I'd been twelve hours ago. Or, at least, her mind had competition. I rolled onto my stomach.

Her fingertips were on my back, and I felt her weight at the edge of the bed. "You obviously love what you do," she said. "It showed last night."

A tingle of anticipation snaked down my legs. "I'm only good when inspired," I said, rolling back over to smile at her.

"Oh, girl, don't ever run for office — you could win." She got up as abruptly as she had sat down. "I absolutely *need* a shower," she said, heading for the bathroom.

I thought to call after her that it bugged me, these insinuations that I was only conning her, sweet-talking in the worst sense of the expression. Because I wouldn't have known how, not with her. Did she think this of me because she was doing it herself? Or was she somehow just incapable of accepting a compliment, feeling she had to make it ricochet off?

I lay there the whole time she was in the bathroom, listening to all the stages of her preparations, hungry for some tossed off revelation of habit when her guard was down. She took only a short shower, then clicked on a blowdryer, then hummed a little — a song I couldn't place — while the sink water went on and off. What nameless friends was she going to meet, I wondered. I felt uneasy not knowing a thing about her daily life, the people she confided in. It was as if I had slipped into some crevice in her life, some unnoticed alleyway, an interruption without context or impact. And I couldn't bear to speculate about what the rest of the weekend might hold, what kind of shambles my own life would be in if I stayed, what kind of black hole of disappointment if I didn't.

"I'm cutting it a little close," she said, emerging from the bathroom wrapped in a white towel. She rummaged in her luggage and pulled out a pair of khaki slacks and a black turtleneck. "Lisa hates it when I'm late," she said, glancing at her watch on the night table. "I'll quit hogging the bathroom for a minute, if you need it."

"I do," I said, leaning over to retrieve my underwear and her borrowed T-shirt from the floor and wrestling quickly into them. I wasn't ready to be so casually naked in front of her. As I was closing the bathroom door, I saw her unwrapping the towel from her body. I felt shy all over again.

I freshened up quickly, saving my shower for later so I didn't have to miss a minute with her. Also, I needed to know now whether she expected me to be gone by the time she got back. She was all dressed when I came out, and was putting blush on in front of the mirror over the desk.

"All yours, again," I said.

She whirled around and smiled wickedly. "You — or the bathroom?"

"Well, the bathroom is a definite," I said. "As far as I go, now it's your turn to take some chances."

She faced the mirror again and smiled at me in the reflection as she continued applying makeup, this time a bit of bronze eyeshadow. "You have a girlfriend, I guess. Of course you would, someone so attractive."

I shrugged, not knowing how to answer, a little dizzy with her compliment. And her comment from last night — about no longer double dealing people — was ringing in my head.

"Can you get free later, and tonight?" she asked. "Do you have to make arrangements?"

I blushed deeply, a result of too many emotions colliding at once. I felt a graze of anger that she simply assumed I'd want to be free, and it was merely a matter of "arrangements." On the other hand, I was thrilled speechless.

"Yes, I can arrange that," I said soberly.

"Good." She was quickly absorbed again by her preparations.

She had no idea, I realized, of the turmoil I'd just made for myself in order to spend another night with her. Unless she did — and didn't care, or figured it was my choice. But was it just another night I was risking everything for? Or was it going to lead to something? And what would that something be — just an interrupted series of hotel weekends? What else was I even hoping for? I considered myself fairly keen at being able to sense a whole range of emotions, of unspoken decisions, from a woman, but Zena Beth seemed to be the quintessential poker face. I had no idea where I stood with her, beyond the fact that having me tonight would amuse her. I wasn't used to that, and I hated it.

"I should be done with lunch by two or so, and then back here after the interview by three-thirty.

Then I thought maybe we could wander down Fifth Avenue — I need to pick up a few things."

Wander down Fifth Avenue — past Gucci, Tiffany's, Steuben Glass, Trump Tower — *to pick up a few things,* as if it were the produce aisle of the A&P. And yet, I really didn't feel she'd said it to sound superior. Wealth had merely become her element, and she was unself-conscious about it.

"Sounds like fun," I said. "What friends are you having lunch with?"

"Oh — Lisa, Lisa Ritz, the singer, and her lover."

"*Lisa Ritz is gay?*" I sputtered.

Zena Beth was closing up her luggage, spritzing on the perfume that made me defenseless. "God, I keep forgetting how young you are. I'm sure everybody at your paper knows. It's an industry secret. I give her a bad time about it constantly, but she won't go on the record. 'No one's ever asked me,' she says. So look, I've got to run. I'll see you back here at three-thirty, then?" Her hand was on the door knob already.

"Yeah, sure," I said, smiling wanly.

She hesitated. "I'd ask you to come to the interview with me, but I thought that would bore you. Or maybe you wouldn't want to be seen with me among other people in your field."

"No, neither, not at all," I said. To be seen with her was part of the thrill. "But I think I'm going to need the time," I said, gesturing vaguely toward the bathroom. In the face of her hesitancy, I didn't want to force the issue.

She came back over to the bed and gently pushed me by the shoulders onto my back. "You will be here when I get back, won't you?" she said, tickling her fingertips along the inside of my thigh as she leaned over me.

"I'll be here," I whispered.

And then she was at the door again, the moment vanished as if it had never happened. "See you," she said as the door shut.

When I got to the office, it was completely deserted. Stripped of its various outrageous personalities, it seemed quite an ordinary newsroom, its beige metal desks pressing against each other at odd angles, its jumble of stacked papers, grimy copy machines and tangled black phone wires all waiting, inertly, for the Monday morning madness. Actually, a few people would be by late tonight, or sometime tomorrow — the theater reviewers and the club columnists who wanted to get a fresh impression down on paper. But this Saturday afternoon, it appeared that the office was all mine.

I got my clothes out of the closet where I'd left them, and took them into the bathroom to change. Then I returned Friday night's clothes there instead, went to my desk and dialed Nikki. She answered on the third ring. The sound of her voice calmed me. Parts of my other life were still intact.

"Joyce! My God, where are you? *How* are you? How was it? Are you flipping out?"

When she stopped firing questions at me, I explained the whole chain of events — holding back the details of our lovemaking, which were too raw and private to share — arriving finally at my present

dilemma. "What in God's name am I going to do?
Should I call Elaine — I mean, I know I have to, but
what am I going to say? You know, the worst of it is
I'd like to enjoy this, just a little bit, but I'm sick
with guilt."

And I was. The moment Zena Beth was out of
the hotel room, I was tortured with images of Elaine
calling my apartment and not finding me home. It
was unbearable. I had nearly left the room with no
intention of going back. Nearly.

"Oh, such trouble," Nikki said. "A woman in
every borough, and one of them famous and filthy
rich. I should have such problems."

"I'm serious," I said. "You've gotta help me."

"Hmmmm, let's see. You're supposed to be with
me, right? So let me think of something harebrained
enough to be typical ..." I heard her tapping
something on the phone, its staccato beat boring into
my brain. "I know — tell her we drove to
Washington, D.C."

"*Washington?* Why would I let you talk me into
going to Washington?"

"A story — a great story for the paper —"

"Wait, this is getting complicated."

"Look, I've got news for you, Joyce. The truth
here isn't much more believable."

"Well, I can't tell her the truth."

"Why not? What if you see Zena Beth again? And
again?"

"I can't think that far." My back tensed. "And if I
ever do tell her, I can't tell her right now, over the
phone."

"I've got it. Just tell her I have relatives in
Delaware and we decided to drive down through the

night. You don't know why. You're twenty-two, that's
why. We got there and collapsed, and you're just
getting up now. And you probably won't be back till
tomorrow."

I considered it. When Nikki said it, so casually
and defenselessly, it had a ring of truth. But I
couldn't imagine myself getting the words out
without sounding as incredulous as I expected Elaine
to be. I was not the kind of person to drive to
Delaware on a lark without an overnight bag, and she
knew it. Still, what choice did I have? Not to call
would have been shocking, a major Richter scale
reading on our emotional landscape.

"Okay," I said. "Let me do it now while I have a
modicum of nerve."

"Be brave," Nikki said, in a tone that could have
sent young women off to war. "And when it's over,
put it out of your mind until you get home. Extra
helpings of guilt won't solve anything."

"Mmmmm," I said. "I'll keep you posted."

I punched in Elaine's number without even
putting the phone back down, afraid I would lose my
nerve. My stomach flip-flopped as the ringing purred
in my ear.

"Hi, I can't come to the phone right now . . ."
her tape machine began. Amazing grace, I thought. I
hadn't even allowed myself to hope for that. I left a
hurried message, sounding apologetic about the rest
of the weekend, and said I'd call as soon as I got in
Sunday night.

I was a horrible person, I concluded, and I
deserved whatever painful things happened to me.

* * * * *

Zena Beth had arranged at the front desk for me
to have my own key to the room, so when I got
back at three-thirty, I started to let myself in. But the
door opened from the inside, and there she was,
smiling broadly.

"Hi," she said, stepping aside to let me in. "My
debating partner was a no-show, so they did a quick
interview with just me. I got done earlier than I
thought."

"Oh," I said. The hard knot of anxiety I'd built
up all morning melted like a pat of butter in a frying
pan at the sight of her.

"Whatd'ya say we storm Fifth Avenue, then?"

The city streets, the actual pavement, comforted
me. I knew my way around, this was my element,
and I understood the cachet of being a native New
Yorker, even if Zena Beth mostly chose to make fun
of Yankees. As we walked, I kept scanning the
crowds to see if she was being recognized. If she
was, no one showed it, in classic New York style.

"How was lunch?" I asked. "How long have Lisa
Ritz and her lover been together, anyway?"

"Oh, God, forever — nineteen years, I think."

I whistled my admiration.

"I know. Helena and I were together three, and
worked every day of it to stay that way."

It had not escaped my notice that Helena Zoë
drifted into nearly every conversation we had. It
occurred to me to do a test — get her talking about
deer lice or something equally unlikely — just to see
how she would manage to introduce her famous
ex-lover to the subject.

We pushed through the revolving glass doors into
Tiffany's first. Zena Beth moved along the rows of

glass counters slowly, inspecting the ruby, diamond and emerald necklaces with the appraising look of someone in the position to afford them. I felt ridiculous trailing along beside her, peering at the glittering jewelry under the hot lights. For one thing, I didn't yet have any kind of love or respect for such jewelry, favoring instead things made of leather or enamel. I associated this kind of display with women I didn't like — wives of rightwing businessmen or overtanned, empty-headed celebrities.

Zena Beth had paused momentarily over a counter that showcasing emeralds, and a saleswoman in a red and black suit surely more expensive than my entire wardrobe was suddenly and wordlessly in front of us. Zena Beth looked up and smiled. "May I see the teardrop necklace?" she asked confidently. "Emeralds are my favorite," she said to me.

"This is really one of our most exquisite pieces," the saleswoman said, tactful enough to include both of us in her glance. Laying the necklace on a black velvet pad, she went on to describe the craftsmanship, where the stones were from and the philosophy behind the design, but I was only half-listening. I watched Zena Beth pick up the necklace and rest it against the palm of one hand.

"Allow me to let you see how it looks on," the saleswoman said, reaching for the necklace.

"No, thank you, another time," Zena Beth said. "I'll be late with my other chores, but I am going to keep it in mind." She laid it back on the velvet pad and we moved briskly away.

"Let's go upstairs to the silver," Zena Beth said. As we were waiting for the elevator, she said, "I used to own one just like it. It was a gift. After we broke up, I couldn't bear to see certain things around. And it didn't hurt to have the cash for it — it let me hibernate in the house for a couple of months, without taking any calls or writing a single word. It was all I was able to do, and it afforded me that luxury. So wherever it is, I'm grateful to it."

I had nothing to say to this, not that the small paneled elevator was the place to say it. I was at a loss to figure out the why of these revelatory bursts. Because after they were said, she seemed done with whatever emotion was associated with them. I sensed that she even preferred me to listen in silence, as if we were in a confessional and I were giving her some kind of silent absolution.

The second floor was far less intimidating — some of the small silver bookmarks and key chains were even in my price range — and as a result, the crush of people was greater and more unruly. Zena Beth made a path for us into the back, and started looking at some silver clocks and picture frames. "A congratulations present for a friend," she said by way of explanation. While she was comparing prices, I moved off to a counter behind her, feeling it would be polite to give her some privacy. I was in no danger of a salesperson coming over to me here, since this counter, with pens and pins and bookmarks, was sufficiently crowded with people aggressively looking for help. An inverted triangle bookmark caught my eye, and I tried to imagine it engraved with my initials. I used the cardboard bookstore bookmarks you got free with your receipt.

"See something you like?" Zena Beth said, suddenly beside me again.

It occurred to me to say I was looking at it —

meaning her — but I didn't. I felt more like I was on
a field trip with a remote professor than out
shopping with the woman I'd just made love to all
night. Her daytime armor was firmly in place. "Didn't
you get anything? Where's your package?"

"I'm having it shipped," she said, as she led us
back to the elevators. "A young friend of mine is
finally getting a play produced. Off-Broadway. With
someone very good. It's a very big break for her."

I wondered spitefully if being friends with Zena
Beth Frazer had something to do with it, but didn't
say so.

"Listen, would you mind if we skipped the rest of
the shopping?" she said when we were out on the
street. "I'm feeling a little worn out all of a sudden.
Actually, I think you're partly to blame."

I ducked my head shyly and felt a spiral of
happiness start at my ribcage and move upward. "Not
at all."

On the way back to the hotel, she asked me
about *Hip* and what stories I'd done and what I
wanted to do with my life.

"The rest of my life?" I asked. "I'd like to run the
place, I guess."

"Then you should. I bet you could. You should
make it happen, plan your moves. But remember, the
only thing worse than not getting what you want is
getting it."

"That's hard to believe."

"Ah, the sweet perspective of youth."

My cheeks burned, and I realized all at once how
aptly the expression applied to my being here with
her. In my fantasies, it never occurred to me that I
might have to risk something, someone, to be with

her. Or that anything or anyone else might mean enough to me to make being with her bittersweet.

Back at the room, she made little pretense about what was on her mind. She took off her leather jacket, and then just kept taking off the rest of her clothes, before throwing back the crisply tucked-in bedsheets. The curtains were still pulled over partway, and the late afternoon sun was pouring a warm and hopeful light into the room. It was my favorite sun, the sun of well-spent afternoons, of ending school days, a pause between the glare of daylight and the intrigue of night.

I sat down on the bed, my back to her, and started to self-consciously kick off my shoes and pull off my socks. Then I felt her behind me, reaching around to unbutton my striped shirt. I held my breath, watching her hands expertly work their way down and pull the shirt cleanly off. Next she disposed of my bra and pants. My legs felt rubbery with anticipation by the time she pulled me back onto the bed and kneeled over me.

Her eyes looked a little wild, her energy level doubled. She touched me with complete confidence, and a new hunger of expectation. She crushed me in a hug with her legs and arms, and I could feel the cultivated strength of her body. Even though she was more petite than I was, it crossed my mind that she could hurt me easily if she wanted to.

But now it was purely pleasure, as if she knew exactly where the pockets of desire lay in wait in my body. Her lips and mouth and tongue were fast and warm on my neck, my ears, my nipples. Heat and chills raked over me; a tremble started in my legs. All the while she whispered and exclaimed, praised and

pleaded, going quiet only when she pushed my legs
apart and pressed her open mouth against me. When
she thrust her fingers inside me, I was catapulted to
some faraway place, tethered precariously to my body
by a fierce and angry pleasure, helpless against the
force of it, lost inside the rush like a surfer in the
circle of a perfect wave, and falling, crashing,
dragging away from the energy slowly, slowly going
calm.

"You're frowning so hard — did I hurt you?" she
murmured into my neck.

"God, no," I said, disoriented and embarrassed. I
had a vague sense that I had been loud and unruly.
One of the pillows was missing.

I turned to her with indefatigable passion. I ran
my palms full up against her, half surprised I didn't
scorch her, half wishing, in fact, that I could in some
way brand her, mark her as my own, as if, in tracing
the dark, silky wetness of her with my tongue, in
pressing my fingers deep within her, I could
somehow fully have her, have her permanently, that
it would not evaporate, that there would be no
separation between us she could tolerate or bear. And
the illusion was complete; she clung to my neck and
back like a needy lover who has, in passion, wrestled
free of her own will. She bucked against me in a
fury of release, and I shut my eyes tightly against her
inner thigh until she was still.

When we pulled away, our bodies sticky with
shared dampness, I saw that it was nearly dark. The
hours had slipped easily by us. I let one hand roam
over her lean stomach and ribs, reluctant to fully
re-emerge, to take our respective corners.

"Hungry?" she asked, snapping on the light. She

looked down at me, smiling mischievously. My heart
leapt. "Not that kind," she said.
"I could eat," I said. "Room service, again? The
help will talk."
"They start talking as soon as they see my name
in the ledger." She dialed.
Jealousy swept over me like a fever. "Am I just
the girl of the weekend, then?" I asked.
"No one who did what you just did to me gets
called a girl," she said. "You're a woman, and a
hot-blooded one at that." Her voice changed as she
gave an order to room service. "I thought you might
be in the mood for steak."
I happened to love steak, but my mind wasn't on
a meal. "You have a not-so-subtle way of not
answering questions," I said.
"So do you. I never got an answer to my
question this morning, about whether or not you
have a girlfriend."
"I thought you'd read between the lines."
"Exactly." She got up and faced the mirror,
smoothing her hair.
"Truce, then. You answer my question first."
She turned around. "For a reporter you weren't
taking very good notes. I told you yesterday it had
been a long time since someone pampered me."
On the contrary, I remembered everything exactly,
more than I was prepared to admit to her. Couldn't
she see what I wanted — reassurance, some dollop of
affection to match even a few degrees of her sexual
enthusiasm? "Being pampered is not the same. You
can have sex without being pampered."
"Ah — so you do more than take notes. You do
instant news analysis, too." She laughed, to take the

edge off what she must have known showed as a
flicker of hostility. There it was, like a pocket of
quicksand on a picturesque beach, ready to catch
your heel when you least expected it.

She sighed, and sat down on the bed. "Honey
child, I haven't got the time, the energy, or the
inclination to bed a different woman every weekend,
or even every month. I only get involved with people
I find interesting. And I've seen a lot of interesting
things in my lifetime. I got lucky when it turned out
you were gay."

"Interesting" was a careful choice of words, but I
decided not to push for clarification. The important
word here was "lucky" — she said she felt *lucky* that
I was gay.

The phone rang, preempting any chance to
pursue the point. "Hello? Oh, well, what a surprise. I
just got in. Nothing much — Sure, sure, yes, bring
the dogs. God knows I haven't seen them in a while,
either."

She didn't need to tell me who it was when she
hung up, but she did, anyway. "That was Helena.
She's in New York — I had no idea. She just tried me
here on a fluke. So she asked if she could come by,
just for a bit, to say hello. She's got the Shar Peis
with her. They belong to us both but she more or
less got custody."

I waited in silence for her to make some apology,
ask some pardon. But nothing came. Perhaps she
really didn't see the awkwardness, blinded as she was
by her own need to see Helena.

"Do you still talk to her often?" I called in to the

bathroom, where she had gone and was splashing water in the sink.

"Well, ever since she's been with Christine it's been hard to get together. She's always on a plane, meeting her here in New York, or meeting her in Europe somewhere if she's on assignment."

I was turning glum, I could feel it. My life was like a hard-boiled egg next to their tri-cheese omelettes.

Zena Beth came out of the bathroom and was putting her clothes back on. I hadn't left the bed yet. "Aren't you going to get dressed?"

I wasn't the one having company, I thought to say, but didn't. Suddenly I felt rash. "Yes. I'd better get going."

She stood stock-still and looked at me. "Don't think — don't leave on my account. Of course, if you want to. Helena will only be here a few minutes. I didn't think it would upset you. There's no reason for it to."

I had no words; actually, I had no right. I got up and put the terry bathrobe on. "There's dinner first, anyway," I said.

As if on cue, there was a knock on the door and a bellhop wheeled in our meal. I felt briefly self-conscious. I wondered what he made of the scene.

She must have sensed that I wasn't much in the mood for talking, so she carried on without me. "My daddy was a gambler. My brothers took care of the farm most of the time, and Daddy traveled. When he'd have a winning streak, we'd live like kings. And then months would go by with nothing. The farm wasn't really income-gathering — just enough to feed the seven of us kids. And I was the only girl, and the youngest, so those other six mouths ate the most heartily."

"What about your mother?" I asked, realizing, between sullen bites, that she was in a rare, forthright mood. Maybe she felt she owed me something for her bad manners or maybe just the prospect of seeing Helena was opening her up. Whatever it was, it wouldn't be soon repeated, I felt sure. So much of her demeanor was colored by the Zena Beth of the present, the one she had created, that her past seemed fabled and ultimately faded. And perhaps she wanted it that way, perhaps she preferred that the private demons and disappointments of her past remain silenced.

"I loved my mother," she said slowly. "She died young. I was barely twenty. We hadn't really come to an understanding. She knew I loved women and she blamed herself. She thought it was some combination of her not having enough time for me when I was little, and my having grown up with all brothers.

"Mothers always blame themselves the most when their daughters defect, of course," she went on. "I tried to get her to take it as a compliment, but she wouldn't have any of that. And the truth is, I don't really think it has a whole lot to do with mothers either way. But that might be arrogant. I always had this idea that I sprang fully formed onto the planet, that my mother was just the carrier." She laughed. "What about you — do you ever think you'll tell your parents?"

"I don't know, really. I mean, we don't talk about

it. They retired to Arizona about a year ago so it's
easy to avoid with the distance. They know I don't
date men. They know I have a lot of women
friends."

"Tell them. How can you stand not telling them?"
she demanded, suddenly irritable. "Are you so unsure
of their love that you couldn't risk it?"

I was stunned for a moment; her criticism hurt
more than I would have guessed. "I don't see how
love is exactly the point," I said when I recovered.
"There are certain things they consider decent
behavior, and certain things they don't. You can love
someone and then find out you have wildly different
values about something important. It doesn't mean
you stop loving them, but you might choose to stop
associating with them."

"No, no I don't believe that." She took her
napkin off her lap and laid it next to her plate. She
looked flushed, as if she didn't trust herself to speak
just then. The force with which she believed things
was exciting all by itself — it was what came through
in her plays and essays and speeches, and here it
was, right across a dinner plate from me. "When you
love, you love completely. You don't get to edit out
the parts about a person that are inconvenient."

There was another knock on the door just then, a
more decisive, less obsequious knock than the
bellhops gave. "Who is it?" Zena Beth called out.

"Me, and Rodgers and Hammerstein," the
unmistakable voice of Helena Zoë called back.

"I'll, uh, go in the bathroom," I whispered.

"Don't be silly. I'm not hiding you." She got up.

"It's not just for your sake. I just don't feel up to
meeting her right at this moment, if that's okay."

There was no misinterpreting the look of relief on
her face. I shut the bathroom door quietly behind
me.

"Hi, stranger," Zena Beth said cheerfully as the
front door opened.

Helena laughed as the dogs whined and
whimpered and stamped their eight feet in greeting.
"Oh, I hope I didn't interrupt your dinner —" she
said.

I heard the dishes clattering around. What was
Zena Beth doing — stacking them so it wasn't
apparent that there had been a place setting for
two?

"I'm glad you could make time to see me,"
Helena said. "I really need to talk, actually." Their
voices moved to the far end of the room and I
couldn't hear every exchange, which was just as well
because I felt smarmy about eavesdropping. Not that
I had much choice, given the close quarters. Actually,
Zena Beth ought to have felt more smarmy, I
thought, and it didn't appear to be stopping her.

I clutched the robe around me peevishly. What
would I do or say if Helena asked to use the john?
Personally, I felt I would be able to sense if someone
else was in a room with me, even if I couldn't see
or hear her. Sometimes you actually could "hear"
someone standing too close to you say, on a train,
when you had your eyes closed. It had something to
do with displacing the energy field near you or some
such. Why wasn't Helena at least half this observant,
I wondered.

It didn't matter; Rodgers and Hammerstein were.
At the base of the closed bathroom door came the
loud sniffing of two black Shar Pei noses. They

sounded as if they could suck up the whole carpet through their nostrils. How was it that Helena remained oblivious? One of the dogs whimpered a little, and then let out a groan as it laid its body flush across the door. Great, I thought, I was being held hostage by an oversized, wrinkly canine.

"Well, you didn't look twice over your shoulder when you left me," Zena Beth was saying. "You barely took the time to pack your underwear. Though I guess that was because you didn't expect to have much use for it where you were going."

My eyebrows shot up into my hairline, but, amazingly, Helena only laughed. Then Zena Beth laughed, too, though I didn't think she'd originally meant the barb to be completely lighthearted.

"It's just not what it used to be," Helena was going on. ". . . either fighting or a million miles away on the phone . . . to be squeezed in like another assignment . . . my own life to lead, too. But she doesn't understand."

"You know what you have to do, darlin'." For some reason, Zena Beth's voice carried a lot further. Or maybe it was because I was so primed to listen for it. "You don't need me to tell you. And I can't push you. I could be said to have ulterior motives."

Helena laughed. There was a pause and then I heard them shuffling toward the door. "I was thinking of becoming a redhead," Helena said. "What do you think?"

"I think it won't change your life," Zena Beth said. They laughed again, the dogs sprang into a frenzy of movement, and then the door closed behind them all.

I waited, my shoulders tensed. But Zena Beth did

not open the bathroom door; I heard her walk back into the room. "You can come out, now, Joyce," she called.

She was sitting on the bed, getting undressed again. Desire raked over me. I could make her forget Helena Zoë, I vowed. Helena Zoë, who couldn't seem to see beyond her own private crises and concerns.

"Thank you," she said when I sat on the bed next to her. "I guess I really did need a few minutes alone with her. It was perceptive of you to notice that. I guess I wasn't as considerate."

I smiled. "It's okay. You can return the favor sometime." I ran my hand down her bare back.

"Oh, I couldn't now, honey," she said, almost flinching. "I'm so tired. I have to get some sleep. My flight's early tomorrow morning."

"I didn't mean that," I protested. "Every time I put a finger on you it doesn't mean I'm trying to get you in a prone position." I tried to laugh but I knew it sounded unconvincing.

"Oh, I guess it just feels that way," she said, curling onto her side.

Now it was her turn to be perceptive.

— 4 —

When I got to the apartment, the light on my tape machine was flashing. One message was from my mother. The other was from Elaine.

"Joyce, it's Saturday, I got your message. I need to know what's going on. Call me when you get in."

The words were few and straightforward, but I could hear in her voice the full range of emotion she had worked herself through: disbelief, anger, fear, pride. Now that I was out of Zena Beth's hotel room, it all seemed like some far-fetched, overheated dream.

This apartment, the woman behind this voice on the tape machine, this was my real life.

I dialed before I had anything ready to say. The fact was, I had been rehearsing various versions of various lies on the subway ride home, knowing I was not going to be able to carry off a single one.

"Hello?" Elaine said on the second ring.

"Hi, it's me," I said. "Let's not talk on the phone. Let's just meet. I can be there in an hour."

There was silence. "So it's not true, then. The trip to Delaware with Nikki. I didn't think so."

"I — I don't want to start this on the phone. Just let me come over."

"Okay." There was no trace of hope in her voice.

I didn't know much about Brooklyn before I met Elaine. My whole New York experience had revolved around Queens, where I grew up and still lived, and Manhattan, the only respectable place to work. A ferry trip to Staten Island during my senior prom does not seem fair to count. But through Elaine, I grew to appreciate Brooklyn like a loud but lovable relative. Elaine introduced me to the narrow, sawdust-floored delis that sold all manner of Italian cold cuts and homemade cheeses and pastas. To the restaurants with their wobbly tables and paintings of Venice and harsh lights — and some of the best food I have ever tasted. To the waterfront neighborhoods with their wholesale fresh lobsters. But a large part of all of its charm, I knew, was having Elaine there to show it to me, allowing me to get caught up in her affection for it.

Now, as I walked down the familiar streets toward her apartment, with their neat and homey brownstones, their not-yet-in-bloom gardens with the statues of the Blessed Mary or St. Jude out front, I felt like I belonged here more than anywhere else. Dread had gathered in a painful knot in my chest. There was little chance that this could go well. I allowed myself a moment of self-pity — no lesbian could have been expected to be able to say no to Zena Beth Frazer. Why couldn't there be a parallel plane of time where I could play out this affair with her without wreaking havoc on my life?

Elaine had the garden apartment of a brownstone, which meant that it was a few steps down to her door. I pressed the front bell slowly. She opened the door and we both smiled a little shyly. The sight of her lush figure in tight jeans, her full lips and dark, kind eyes hit me with a fresh impact.

"Did you have lunch, yet?" she asked. The apartment was fragrant with spicy sauce.

"No, but I'm not really up for food."

We sat down on the overstuffed maroon couch in the tiny living room that doubled as a darkroom. Black and white prints leaned against every bit of available wall space on the far side of the room. But she kept the other side spotless and cozy with bookshelves and a reading lamp.

"No, the story about Delaware isn't true," I began. "But I just couldn't tell you before I left, and I really couldn't tell you on the phone yesterday. So I'm coming a little late to the truth."

I could see her steeling herself for the worst, but she certainly couldn't have anticipated the Zena Beth Frazer element of the story. By the time I finished,

she looked like she might have laughed if I didn't
look so serious.

"Your lies go from bad to worse," she said.

"It sounds crazy, I know, but it's true. This is
probably lousy consolation, but I would never have
done this, to you or to us, if it hadn't been who it
was. It's just, I mean, the thing I fantasized about —
without the slightest hope that it could ever happen
— since I was a kid. I would never, ever have done
this if it was just some other woman. But Zena Beth
— I mean, it wasn't even in the realm of ordinary
emotions, like, 'Do I like this person?' " I stammered.
"It was something else entirely, like ... I mean, I
have nothing else to compare it to, even ..."

I stopped talking when I saw that she had started
to cry. She was sitting very still with her hands
folded in her lap, her head tilted forward slightly,
eking out stingy tears. What made it all so much
more unbearable was that I had always been her
comforter, and now I was the one hurting her.

It took only a second before she was in my arms,
her face flush against my chest, giving in fully to
sobs. My own eyes burned but the full force of my
grief stayed locked in place, a dense, dark, bitter
lump of remorse. It didn't seem fair to cry for myself
now, and yet, ultimately, it was impossible not to.

We both cried till our cheeks grew tight and our
eyes puffy, and the whole while, a fist of doom
squeezed tight around my heart. At any moment, I
was sure, Elaine would recoil from me, having
regained herself enough that she would realize she
was actually clinging to the enemy. But she didn't.
Instead, she looked up and kissed me, unleashing a
longing in me that was deeper, more grounded, more

well-seasoned and tender than anything I'd felt all weekend. She stood up and took my hand, leading me in to her bedroom.

Her body seemed new and fresh after the separation. She was long and lush and amply curved; her breasts had the weight and fullness that never failed to stir me. I pressed my face into her cleavage, dewy already with our efforts, and inhaled the scent of her, salty and sweet, powdery and woody all at once. I gathered her thick long hair to one side and ran my tongue down the strained tendons of her neck. We kissed till our lips were bruised and slippery.

"Tell me you'll never see her again, never even think of her again," Elaine whispered into my neck, "and we'll pretend that none of it ever happened."

It took a moment before the full impact of what she was saying dawned on me. "Do we have to talk about this now?"

"There's no better time to talk about it." She pulled away and leaned up on one elbow.

I rolled onto my back and stared at the ceiling, fighting off panic. I had tried and tried to make loving Elaine enough to make me able to renounce Zena Beth, but there it was, some crazy strain of virus that weakened all my good intentions, that seemed to force me to hurt myself and this woman I loved and wanted. I saw Zena Beth's face at the elevator, revealing one of her rare moments of vulnerability, saying, "I'll call you when I get there." I wanted that. I wanted that, too. I sat up, my back to Elaine, and put my head in my hands.

"You can't do it, can you?" Elaine said evenly. "Get out, then. Just take your clothes and get out."

"Do we have to be rash?" I asked, whirling around. "I mean, isn't there some way —" I was desperate now, and soon not to be in control of my voice.

"I won't share you. Not after all this time. It's insane. This thing with her is hopeless, anyway. I would never have believed you could be such a fool. And vain, too. Because I know you can't love her. You're not one of these infantile women who thinks she's in love after one good lay. You're just bursting with ego. It's sickening, actually."

I started to cry again. I felt stripped raw, as if she had peeled away a layer of skin and was blasting me now with a hose. It could have been the truth, everything she was saying. I couldn't tell, but I was humiliated, anyway. With Zena Beth, I felt that I might lead a different life — a bigger, more glamorous one than I had ever allowed myself to imagine. And I wasn't able to give that up.

I couldn't bring myself to say any of this to Elaine. She didn't want my reasons. She wanted my fidelity or nothing. And I knew that she wouldn't have been the woman I loved and respected if she hadn't made the terms so absolute.

"I can't bear the thought of not seeing you —" I broke off, and began again with great effort. "It's not right . . . Isn't there some way . . . ."

"Get out, Joyce. Now. Please," Elaine said.

And because her voice had moved from anger to grief, had arrived at the soft wall of sadness where I might have been able to fight unfairly, to make her back down, I gathered up my clothes, dressed quickly in the living room, and left.

* * * * *

I had put my tape machine on to ward off having to talk to my mother. "This isn't a good time, Ma," was not a sentence I had ever used to successfully deter her from a monologue. She would be worried — nearly a week had passed since she'd left her last message — but I had no choice. I couldn't talk to her now.

I lay on my bed, limp with misery and self-hatred. I prayed for Elaine to call, and prayed for her not to call. Because I knew if she called, it would be only to see if *I* had changed *my* mind, because I knew she would not change hers. And I didn't have whatever it was that I needed — courage, character, guts — to change mine.

I called Nikki and relived the whole gruesome scene. She listened thoughtfully to the end, sucking on a cigarette periodically; I could hear the reassuring "puup" of her lips on the filter. "Girl, I only hope I get laid as much on my good days as you do on your bad."

"Please stop," I said, laughing briefly despite myself, and then feeling worse. "This is it. I mean, I blew the whole fucking thing. Zena Beth will never call me again, and Elaine's gone now, too, and for what?"

"Joyce, old friend, haven't you ever heard the word reconciliation?"

"Forget it," I said. "How could we go back? It's like the Garden of Eden after the serpent. If you could hear how she hates me. She'll never feel the same way for me —"

"The same isn't always the best, or the only. There's the new, the recombined."

"Forget it. You don't know her like I do. If I went back, she'd know it was because Zena Beth came to nothing. And how low could you go? She'd hate herself. I don't think I'd even give her the option."

"Hmmmm. Very noble. Actually I think it's you who're afraid how you'd feel about her if she *did* take you back. Because you still confuse forgiveness with spinelessness."

"I don't confuse them. I can tell them apart. Not everyone can." I was really being mean now, because I knew Nikki would know I was referring to her last doomed affair, in which she forgave the woman all kinds of outrageous transgressions. But I was wounded and bleeding, ready to strike out on all sides. I loved Nikki because she knew this, and didn't strike back. She sucked deeply on her cigarette, and I thought of how she looked when she smoked: vastly sophisticated, mysterious, elegant, all the things the tobacco industry wanted you to think. All my desires were wrong-headed these days.

"I think what you have to do now," Nikki said, exhaling authoritatively, "is hang up and let Zena Beth Frazer call you, like she said she would."

It was a nice try. I thanked Nikki and hung up.

A shrill, insistent ring jostled me from a deep and jagged sleep. There had been dreams with snarling dogs and mutated people. I knocked the phone off

the bedstand but managed to put the receiver in the
right configuration to my face. "Hello?" I croaked.

"Joyce? Is that you?" It was that one-of-a-kind
Southern accent. I sat bolt upright.

"Zena Beth? My God, are you in San Francisco
already? What time is it?"

"I've been here several hours, actually. The
wonder of time zones. It's about nine your time. I'm
afraid I woke you up."

I rubbed my free hand roughly over my eyes and
forehead. "No, no, it's fine. I mean, yes, you woke
me up, but I'm up now."

She laughed. "You're adorable when you're
confused."

My heart nearly leapt from my chest. She was
taking advantage of me with my guard down,
smoothing over my rough edges with her sly
compliments. I knew this, but they affected me,
anyway. "How was your flight?" I thought it best to
concentrate on something neutral and uncomplicated.

"Fine, except I couldn't sleep, couldn't work. I
kept thinking about your ample talents."

A hot blush rendered me fully awake. "Ah, too
bad."

"I feel a little guilty," she said. "I don't think I
was very entertaining, keeping you holed up in a
hotel room."

"It would have been indecent to do what we
were doing anywhere else."

She laughed, and then her tone turned thoughtful.
"I'm sorry about the thing with Helena." There she
was, making her expected appearance, in record time
this conversation. "I called a friend of mine back

home — to tell her about the interesting young woman I spent the weekend with — and when I told her about Helena coming up and you going into the bathroom and the whole mess, she said I was lucky you hadn't tossed me out the window. It was really very gallant of you."

"Well, I didn't take it personally," I lied.

"There are things I want you to take personally, though," she said. "I don't just call up women and haul them into bed. But you, uh, turned out to be pretty irresistible."

Soon, I feared, I would be floating along the ceiling. I made some kind of demurring noises.

"I wanted to know if I could send you some airline tickets so you could come down and visit Mountville this weekend," she said, sounding — it was true, I wasn't just imagining it — shy and nervous. "Would you be able to?"

For a second I thought of Elaine and what in the world I would tell her, but then, with a heavy heart, I realized there was no need. I had made my choice. "Sure, yes, I can do that. I'd love to. But about the tickets —"

"Don't be silly. It's my treat. I'll send them overnight mail. Kennedy airport good for you?"

"Yes, perfect." I was a little dazed by how fast she was moving.

As if she were reading my mind, she said, "I thought it would be nice if we got to know each other a little better."

* * * * *

Getting through the work week proved to be alternately harder and easier than I thought. Some afternoons, I was buried deep in phone calls and I'd look up to see that it was swiftly six o'clock. Other days, the hours crept along, and everything seemed to remind me of Elaine or Zena Beth and I would feel stalked by different kinds of terror.

Zena Beth called on Tuesday at the office to make sure the tickets had arrived safely, which they had, but we were both rushed so the conversation was strictly informational. She would have a car waiting for me at the airport when I arrived Friday night, and the driver would have instructions to take me out to her farm, about an hour away.

Every morning I touched the tickets and studied them, not quite believing they were real. Sometimes I would fall into a time warp, and, in my excitement, went to call Elaine and exclaim how strange life really was. Then I would relive the whole breakup and feel the blackness of loss all over again.

When I got home Thursday night, I set about packing. When the phone rang I snatched it up.

"Joyce? It's Elaine."

Adrenaline pumped through my veins. "Elaine . . . how are you?"

"Well, I've been miserable, frankly, and hoping you have been, too."

"I have." It was true half the time, anyway. No, it wasn't like that. I was both miserable all the time, and thrilled all the time. The feelings overlapped and infected each other; they would not stay in their own tidy, separate spheres.

Her tone picked up a little. "I thought maybe we could get together tomorrow night, to talk, to see if maybe things could work themselves out." She meant, to see if Zena Beth had blown me off yet.

"Oh — tomorrow, actually, I can't. I mean, normally I would but this weekend, I, well I'll actually not be...." I was pathetic.

"Jesus, I'm so stupid. You're going to see her again this weekend, aren't you? Yeah, miserable — I'll bet you are. Just forget I called. Please, forget it." And then she hung up, leaving the line buzzing in my ear.

I knew she wouldn't call again. If there had been any glimmer of hope, that had killed it. That had been her maybe-I'm-being-rash/should-give-her-more-credit/was-too-hard-on-her-last-weekend call. Now I had totally humiliated her. It was, finally, the last unforgivable thing.

I held the phone for a long time, not sure at all that I was heading into the arms of the right lover. Without thinking, I dialed Elaine right back. I had no clue what I was going to ask or say or beg or promise. But I didn't get a chance. The line was busy. And it stayed that way all night.

— 5 —

We drove through nearly pitch blackness for over an hour before the driver, a thin, silent man, pulled up a long, pebbled driveway and came to a stop. We could have been anywhere at all for all I knew or could see, and my New York paranoia kicked into high gear. I sat rigidly in the back seat waiting for his next move. He had the advantage. This could have been where he dumped and abandoned me, or had his way with me.

"This is the Frazer residence, Miss," he said pleasantly, getting out and holding the door open for

me. Then he opened the trunk and handed me my
bag. "Fee's all taken care of, Miss. I'll just wait here
till you're safely inside." He gestured toward a front
porch I was able to make out only because of a
small light by the door.

"Oh, thank you very much," I said. I saw that he
was not only perfectly harmless, but nice. The sinister
outlines of the scene fell away. He smiled
encouragingly as I went to the door and rang the
bell.

An elaborate chime sounded, and shortly I heard
steps coming closer. It seemed miraculous, but there
stood Zena Beth Frazer, framed against the warm
glow of her kitchen, holding the door open for me.

"Hi, come in, without the night-flying critters,"
she ordered. "Thank you!" she called past me to the
retreating driver. He tooted the horn in reply.

She took my bag. I watched her in her jeans and
black and white-checked shirt, the collar of which
was turned up fetchingly, and waited for some
embrace of greeting. Instead, she just smiled briefly.
"So, the flight and the drive went uneventfully, I
hope."

I saw that she had on quite a bit less makeup
than last time I saw her. She looked more earthy,
more relaxed on her own turf. I longed to kiss her,
to take her hungrily in my arms, but I didn't dare.

"Well, this is my place, be it ever so humble,"
she said.

She paused so I could look over the first floor —
a living room with a piano and fireplace, a library
with floor-to-ceiling books, a small gym, her writing
room. Nothing was garish or flashy; it was all rather

retiring, unremarkable even, with several key details revealing the extent of her means. Many of the books, for instance, appeared to be leather-bound collector's editions, or antiques. All the gym equipment was top of the line. "I'll give you a decent tour in the morning," she said, leading us up the stairs. "Right now, I'll let you get some sleep. Here's your room," she said, hitting a light switch.

It was a sweet room, done in maroon and pink, with a shiny wood floor covered partially with a black and pink oriental rug. But I took an instant dislike to it, because she had called it "mine." Did she think I had traveled all this way to sleep alone? Why was she acting like the bed and breakfast innkeeper? Where was the woman who, a mere week ago, had called me irresistible? I must have been standing there, blinking and frowning, because finally she asked what was wrong.

It could have been the trip, the stress of the week, Elaine, everything, because suddenly I felt near tears, and as soon as I realized it, I was furious with myself. "Nothing," I said, regaining my equilibrium. "It's just, I thought —"

"You don't have to sleep in here, honey," she said, catching my hand loosely. "But the house is big enough that you can unpack in here, have some space."

I tightened my grip on her hand and gathered my nerve. "I heard stories about warm Southern welcomes," I said, smiling tentatively. Had she changed her mind about me since last we met?

She took a step back. "Hot-blooded — I wasn't wrong about that." She returned my smile. "I'm a

set-in-my-ways old lady, you'll see. I need a little time
to get used to you again, to get used to your being
here. It's the first time —"

She didn't have to finish; I could guess. The first
time some other woman had been in her house since
Helena Zoë left. At least this time she'd had the
courtesy not to say her name.

"You can use this bathroom," she said, showing
me across the hall to a narrow, old-fashioned,
white-tiled bathroom. "Anything you see that you
need to use, feel free. Blowdryer, what have you. Be
less to unpack that way. I'll just be downstairs
finishing up some bills." She smiled again and went
down.

I stood in the room, paralyzed by indecision. Did
she expect me to take a shower? I didn't feel up to
it and everything seemed foreign and unwelcoming. I
unpacked a few things and arranged them on top of
the dresser. Then I kicked off my shoes and sat on
the bed, trembling.

What kind of jerk had I just made of myself,
yanking on her hand like she was some kind of
dairymaid? What had I expected, a reunion like
something out of *Gone With the Wind*? She was a
grown woman, a famous, wealthy, well-traveled one
with a string of famous lovers, and what was I? Some
kid with an entry-level job.

I took a few deep breaths until the tremble
subsided. Then I closed the door and got undressed
— there didn't seem to be any alternative I could
think of. I carefully smoothed out the turquoise silk
nightshirt I had bought just for this trip. I felt
ridiculous in it; at home I wore men's pajama tops,
and with Elaine, I had worn nothing.

I went to the top of the landing and tried to figure out what to do next. There was no sound at all from downstairs. It didn't seem like a good idea to parade down in a silk nightshirt if she had been skittish around me fully dressed. "Need any help down there?" I called out finally, wincing at the lameness of my ruse.

I heard her snap out a lamp and walk leisurely toward the stairs. At the bottom, she smiled up at me. "You look absolutely edible in that color," she said. I blushed all the way to my scalp.

She came up the stairs and turned right, motioning for me to follow her down the hall. She turned a dimmer, throwing a soft, warm light over what I took to be the master bedroom. A king-sized bed against the near wall, up on a platform, faced a huge bay window. A beautiful antique mirror hung on another wall covered in tapestry wallpaper, and other walls bore paintings of horses and riders, some from the Civil War period, it appeared. A magnificent dark wood dresser stood in the far corner. She flicked another switch and classical music could be heard, faintly. She allowed me a moment to take it in, and I could feel her beaming lovingly at it herself.

"It's great," I said.

"Thank you. Make yourself at home. I'll be right back."

I sat on the bed — the only other choice was a chaise lounge in the shadows at the far end of the room — and waited tensely for her to return. She had sufficiently thrown me off so that I didn't know what to expect, or what she expected of me. I took in the room again slowly.

The whole house was nothing like what I had

expected. There was an understated country flavor
about it, a modest, well-made simplicity. It didn't
seem at all like the flashy, arrogant Zena Beth Frazer
of the red silk dresses. Could that all be a cultivated
persona? Was the real Zena Beth someone else
entirely?

She came back in, wearing a long, black silk robe.
When she closed the door, I saw that the robe had
an elaborate colorful dragon on the back.

"Is that from Japan?"

"Yes. It's a fascinating country." She sat on the
bed next to me, looking almost apologetic. Then she
reached up and pushed my hair behind one ear. "I
hope I don't seem cold to you. I'm just a bit of a
misanthrope. I get reclusive out here. It takes me a
little time. But I'm very glad to see you. You're —"
She stopped herself, and then, tilting my face toward
hers with two fingers under my chin, she kissed me
lightly on the lips. Desire raced through me like a
fever.

We got up so she could pull back the quilt, and
then she turned the dimmer off completely. From
somewhere outside — the moon, the stars? — light
washed in through the windows. I watched her, in
silhouette, as she slipped out of her robe and hung it
on the back of the door. When she slid under the
covers and reclined on her back, looking up at me, I
was through with trying to second-guess what she
wanted of me. All I knew was that I was dizzy with
desire and she was here, under me, cool and naked
and still.

When I leaned down to kiss her, she pulled the
nightshirt off over my head. My heart began to race.

Had she been being coy, then? Had she dreamed about this moment, too, underneath all her mannered and reserved ways?

I was suddenly frantic for her, grazing my lips over the length of her, tracing my fingertips lightly down her legs to raise goosebumps, tangling my hands in her hair and licking circles around her ears and nipples. She made small whimpering noises, as if I were hitting her with glancing blows, but she made no effort to defend herself, and instead kept trying to catch me and clutch me to her.

Then, in one neat, effortless move, she turned me onto my back, one arm hooked behind my neck to hold me against her shoulder, and the other palm pressing, pumping gently at my groin. "Oh, you get so wet for me," she breathed into my ear. "I can't resist you when you get like this." My will was completely given over to her, as I felt her fingers thrust powerfully inside me in a flash of heat. A sound I'd never heard myself make before escaped from my throat, and she kept up a relentless dance between my legs, a chaotic swirl of fingers inside me. I was parched and dizzy and nearly crying in frustration before she corralled all her movements into one forceful gesture that sent me over the edge, skidding, the long distance down to some temporary peace.

Temporary because, before the last breath was even over, she moved down and pushed my knees apart and covered me with her mouth. I tried to memorize the motion of her tongue, the flickers and feints that, finally, suddenly, nearly made me double over with the intensity of release.

This time I was leveled. I lay with my arms outstretched, trying to make sense of the room, of what had just happened. Zena Beth was stretched out alongside me, leaning rakishly over me on one elbow. Vaguely I registered that with one leisurely finger she was tracing lines along my thighs.

"I'm sorry. I don't seem to be able to stop myself. You have yourself to blame."

Even in my defenseless state, I felt caution stir. What did she mean by these teasing statements? Was she really the lonely lesbian in self-imposed exile, who got her hands on a willing woman too infrequently? Or were these words really meant for me, and did they spring from any place more personal than sexual passion? I felt in some way that she was behind glass, that I could see her, but not reach her.

I slipped my hand along the back of her neck and pressed her mouth to mine, wanting to blot out these doubts with languid kisses, kisses that were entire songs, chorus after chorus, till I felt she couldn't possibly keep any secrets from me. She shifted on top of me, taking my thigh between her own, and began a gentle, rhythmic motion. In just a few moments, she squeezed hard, shuddered briefly, and moved her head to rest against my shoulder.

"Trying to sneak one in, eh?" I said, wriggling free. "I won't let you off the hook that easily."

"Somehow, I didn't doubt you would," she said lazily, happily.

I knelt over her and opened my mouth on her fully, nearly tearful at her sweetness. I hugged her hip tightly with one arm as I pressed deep inside her, all the while feeling heat rise off her in waves, hearing the angry urgency of her breathing, as I detoured and postponed her pleasure, circling back to find her ever more highly strung and ready, till the last, unsuspecting flicker unleashed a cry from her, made her grip my shoulders almost painfully, and then relax into stillness.

I moved back up and pressed light, feather kisses into her neck. "Mmmmm," she said, arching her back, "there's no after-play with you – it's all foreplay. But this is the country. We get up early here. We have to get some sleep."

I laughed but obeyed, and let her nestle into my side to wait for sleep. The core of me was heavy with fatigue and satisfaction, but I felt a layer of wakefulness on top of that, an anxious, uncertain tug that kept me alert.

I listened as her breathing slowed, and acknowledged what was missing. Except for the last time, Elaine and I had always said we loved each other afterward, flushed and tender with our shared passion. Now the phrase lurked around the outskirts of my consciousness, knowing it was not appropriate, not summoned, not welcome.

In the middle of the night, I woke up, straining my eyes in the darkness to make out something familiar. She had turned away from me, and my arms were wrapped around her from behind. I rolled over and she whimpered faintly in her sleep.

The night is a shroud, I thought, a whole other time zone, where we face our darkest terrors or most inconceivable hopes. Lying in Zena Beth's bed, I felt both: whatever would it mean to share a life with her? And then a stirring of optimism from some deep center of myself: I wanted to find out, more than anything.

— 6 —

I woke up to a warm, empty bed. Morning sun blanketed the room, softening the outlines of everything. I threw on my nightshirt and followed the scent of eggs and coffee down the stairs and into the kitchen. Zena Beth stood in front of the stove, tending to an omelette pan.

"Good morning, Rip Van Winkle," she said. "I believe you alluded last night to the notion of Southern hospitality. I want you to know I *never* cook for myself."

"You should have me over more often, then,

because it smells delicious. What time is it?" I went over and kissed her lightly on the back of the neck.

"About nine. I've been up since six-thirty. Did my workout, showered, answered some letters. And still you slept on," she said, glancing over her shoulder to smile at me.

"To quote another line from last night, you have only yourself to blame."

"Go ahead, sit down, it's just about ready," she said, filling our plates with the omelette, tomato slices, bacon and a corn muffin.

"Now I *know* you don't make breakfast for yourself. There's no way you could put away a meal like this every morning and stay as slim as you are."

"Thanks for saying so, but at my age I have to work at it. The whole system goes downhill after thirty. I know, it's hard for you to believe that at your age. See, you've got room to grow yet, and you're young enough that it's completely natural. Like a colt."

This prompted discussion of her horses, which she talked about with loving maternal attention and pride. Some she showed and some she raced, and those were out on the road now. Two, Atlantis and Ziegfeld, were just for pleasure, and lived on the farm with her year round. She promised to introduce me later.

"But first I thought I'd show you around the neighborhood. Of course, I suggest you get changed," she said, sipping her coffee.

I took the hint and went upstairs to get showered and dressed.

* * * * *

We spent several hours driving around the countryside in her white Jaguar. Both were beautiful. Though it was still drizzling and chilly in New York, April in North Carolina was spring in nearly full bloom. The grass was a new green, and stretched clear out to the horizon. The air was rich with the smells of tobacco and soybean farms, freshly turned earth, dogwood, sunshine. The car purred effortlessly along the narrow, hilly roads, and I could feel Zena Beth holding back on the speed so that I could enjoy the scenery.

She pulled the car onto a smaller road, and soon we were driving through a densely forested area. I could feel the temperature drop and rolled up my window a bit. I kept it open enough that I could hear the leaves rustling and the pines swooning, and what I imagined were the rummagings of countless animals, small and large. "God, it really is beautiful. Makes you wonder why anyone likes to live in cities."

"Agreed," she said, meditatively.

The whole ride she had been quiet. I couldn't tell if the surroundings had a sedative effect on her, or if they triggered memories she didn't care to share. Instinct told me she was feeling distant and prickly, and I was growing weary of the incongruity, that only for certain occasions would she allow herself to be vulnerable. Or was it that in bed she was able to let her emotions recede, absorb into some safe center where they lay dormant?

"When you lived with Helena," I asked carefully, "did you live in this same house?"

She moved her hands further up the wheel, so that I could see her knuckles working as she gripped it. "No, we had a much bigger one, an estate, actually, further up in the mountains where there's skiing. The Smokies are over six thousand feet high at some points, and it can get pretty cold in the winter."

I shifted uncomfortably. It was as if the air in the car crackled with some high-frequency warning.

"When she left, I couldn't afford the upkeep on a place that size, even with my income. Plus it was up in God's country. I mean, I'm a country girl, and I don't like most of mankind, that's true, but when you get that high up in the mountains it's a challenge to function, even with the little things. I couldn't afford the staff to make it convenient, the way it was when we had it together."

She frowned into the distance. "We tried to divide things up evenly, but with any divorce, people get nasty over money. I took a bath on some things, just so we didn't have to keep arguing. I knew that if we kept at it, there wouldn't be any chance of salvaging a friendship, and that was more important to me than the money. I was the one who made the compromises to keep some connection alive. Maybe it was stupid. But I do still hope we might get back together someday."

It would be a lie to say she had kept this any big secret, to say she hadn't hinted about it in a million different ways, made the reality of it a condition even, of our getting to know each other. But hearing it now was like being jolted with an electric probe. Every nerve-ending in my body felt as though it were exposed, and I looked away, out the passenger window, so she wouldn't see my face scarlet with anger and humiliation.

"It's scary, when all is said and done, to love a woman that much. I never want to do it again."

The knife was in, and twisted. My vision blurred slightly, and I bit my lip to keep control of myself. I stopped when I tasted the salty warmth of blood. A slight stirring of nausea rippled through me.

"I thought we'd stop here," she said, pulling the car onto a pebbled road. "There's a clearing, and a campground, and a pretty spectacular view of the mountains if we walk further up."

I allowed myself to be distracted by the scenery, by the complicated thickness of the forest all around us. The smell of pine was dense and intoxicating. But her confession was like an ugly blot on my happiness. Did she mean it as a warning? Or was it just simply the truth, not something she meant to wound with, not even something whose effect she bothered to calculate? Just a neutral statement about life as she lived it?

She parked the car next to some jeeps and vans, and we walked slowly through the nearly empty campground. "Something tells me you're not the camping type," she said.

"Not unless there's an electrical outlet nearby," I said, forcing myself to sound at ease.

Ahead was a clearing and then a rocky incline. Zena Beth moved easily, taking long strides with the unself-conscious surefootedness of a horse. I trailed behind, testing each rock with my sneaker before putting my full weight on it. I saw that we were edging our way along a cliff, and slowly, in increments, a long, jagged stretch of the Smokies moved into full view.

"My God," I whispered.

"There are lots of spots along here where you can find your own private lookout," she said, sitting down. "No nickel viewfinders trashing things up."

"Ah, yes, capitalism."

"Don't get me wrong — I'm all for it. I like the way I live. I would still write if I never got paid a dime for it, but being paid lets me do it all the time. I know that's a privilege. My parents never thought I did an honest day's work, ever. To them, if you didn't sweat, it wasn't work."

I laughed. "It *is* hard to picture you with parents. Did you ever think about being a parent yourself?"

She squinted into the horizon. "I admit I'm basically not selfless enough to do that. Though if I were ever with a woman who really wanted to, I'd probably go along. As long as I didn't have to be the one with the expanding uterus." She picked up a small rock and weighed it in her hand. "But anyway, you're always drawing me out. What about you? Where do your parents think you are this weekend?"

"With Elaine — I mean, with . . . well, they think she's a friend." I'd finally placated my mother with a phone call just before I left.

"Ah, yes. The girlfriend."

"Not any more, just for the record." I was blushing hotly now, feeling like Peter denying Christ.

"Oh, I'm sorry to hear that."

Of all the possible responses she might have made, this was not the one I was most hoping for. "I only mention that because it's true, as of recently. I didn't mean to make you feel — I mean, there isn't —"

She held up her hand. "It's fine. I understand

perfectly. I am sorry, though. These things are never easy."

I nodded, afraid to speak. I hammered two rocks together, to drown out my thoughts. The thing I wanted most to say was impossible: I'm sorry, too, but aren't *we* together, now? *Aren't* we?

"I seem to make trouble for people, long before they get a chance to decide if I'm worth it. Before I was with Helena, she was very discreet. Everyone knew she was gay — it wasn't as though she was fooling anyone — but she never did anything very overt. Then, when she started bringing me to her tournaments and exhibitions, the press dropped all their inhibitions, too. I don't think she was ready for that level of exposure. Of course, it was just innuendo in the papers. But the damage was done. She lost a lot of key endorsement money, because of me, I'm sure of it."

I banged the rocks together a little harder and said nothing.

"Well, let's head into town, shall we? We might be up for some lunch in a little while."

It was close to four by the time we got back to the farm. Zena Beth put the car away and then, as promised, we headed over to the stable to meet her horses.

"Stand on this," she instructed, pointing out a little stump not far from the stable door. It looked to me as though I'd be lucky enough to get both feet on it at once, let alone balance there. "I'm going to let them out — they'll be eager for a run — and they won't bother you if you're elevated a bit. Go ahead on up," she said, as she headed to the stable door.

I felt ridiculous up on the stump. It seemed both ludicrous that the horses might stampede me for no reason, and equally ludicrous that being twelve inches off the ground would be enough to stop them if that really was their intention. But there was clearly no questioning Zena Beth on this point.

I could hear her in the darkness of the stable making cooing noises of the kind one might make with a puppy or a baby, and in the next second, two immense horses came bolting out the doors. My heart clattered in my throat and I fought the urge to charge in the opposite direction. Instead, I stood stock-still in fear as they pounded the ground not ten feet from me and made a carefree turn up the hill and off onto the surrounding hillside. One was a glossy chestnut color, and the other nearly blue-black. I felt moved watching them run — it was easy to see why so many people thought they were the most beautiful of all animals.

Zena Beth, her hands on her hips, watched them gallop out of view. She looked both pretty and handsome in her corduroy shirt, her snug jeans tucked into elaborately marked black and gray cowboy boots. "They won't be back for a good hour. It's safe to come down." She waved me over to the stable.

Inside, the air was dense with the smell of horses and hay, and beams of sunlight fell, as if by design, into each of their stalls. Zena Beth pointed out the different saddles she used, explaining the kind of care the horses required.

"A lot of people say horses are dumb, but I always find those to be people who've never owned them. Horses aren't like other animals — they don't respond to you just because you're a human being. You really have to work at a relationship with them. And if you respect them — treat them well and ride them well — they'll do anything for you. It's absolutely true. But there's no such thing as forcing yourself on a horse." She kept walking around the stable, as if she were reluctant to leave.

"How do you get them back from their run?"

"Oh," she said, laughing. "I don't get them back. They come back by themselves. They know their way, know the hour. You'll see. I can set my watch by them. Do you ride at all?"

"No, I never have, actually."

"Hmmmm, maybe over time. But they wouldn't be fond of a beginner."

"As in most things in life," I said, laughing.

"No, not always. I've always liked being with women who were new to their identity, their sexuality. There's something very exciting about that, seeing it unfold."

And leaves you very much in control, I thought. I looked at her now, in the half light of the stable, with her swarthy, chiseled good looks and her cool, detached air, and felt an irrational, almost violent longing. If only I knew how to break through, I could wash away the flashes of casual cruelty she was capable of.

I slipped one arm around her waist and held the back of her head with my other hand, kissing her hard and long till she stopped trying to gently push me away. She yanked open the snaps of my jacket and rubbed her hands vigorously over my breasts till my nipples were painfully tense and tingling.

"This *isn't* a good idea," she said, pulling away and nearly escaping. "Let's at least go inside."

"No time," I said, my lips parted against her neck. I pushed her carefully but firmly against the dark wall and unzipped her jeans, working them easily down over her slim hips.

"This *really* isn't —" she started to say, but speech degenerated into moans as I moved my hand down past the soft mound of hair to find her warm and moist.

My heart leapt in joyful surprise — here was the incongruity again. All the while she was protesting, some force within her was responding, priming herself for me, for this, at least, for this movement now she was making to meet my hand, so that we moved together as one effort, toward one goal.

I pushed her legs further apart with my knee, feeling my own legs growing unsteady as I absorbed every sound and scent of her. My own groin was pounding, my own throat constricting, as she clung to my neck and fired tiny dart-like kisses up and down my neck and cheeks and ears. I shut my eyes tight against her hair and felt the universe shrink to just this one sensation, the feel of her against my palm, a trickle of her wetness moving past my fingers down the inside of her thigh.

"Oh, God, there —" she gasped, as I deliberately slid just past the place I knew she meant. "Please, *please*," she groaned, angling herself against my fingers. Then, with one sharp, agonized cry, she gave way, her knees buckling slightly, the weight of her upper body shifting against me.

I held her close till her breathing calmed and she pulled away to look at me. "If you're half as hot as I was," she whispered, lightly kissing my face, "you must be dying about now." She started to pull my blouse free of my jeans.

"No," I said, catching her wrist. "I can wait. As long as it takes." And I left her that way, in the shaded dampness of the barn, and walked into the sunlight, straining into the horizon for a glimpse of Ziegfeld and Atlantis returning.

— 7 —

The rest of the evening was quiet. We ate dinner — a meal pre-prepared by her cook which she had only to heat in the microwave — and then we watched some television in the den. She sat on the floor between my legs, leaning against my torso, and occasionally made little purring noises as I absent-mindedly played with her hair. There was something about the ordinariness of these events that was more exciting to me than any extravaganza she might have planned. I allowed myself to fantasize this as our daily life, to hope that she was trying to imagine me as part of her routine.

Sometime late in the evening — it must have been after ten — the phone rang, and she took it in her office. I completely lost interest in the murder mystery we were watching, although I had been fairly caught up. Now I was anxious instead only for some clue about who was keeping her on the phone so long, so late.

The show had ended and the news had come on by the time she came back into the room. She sat down on the floor again, but this time nearly a couch-length away. She kept her gaze fixed on the television, and didn't even ask who had been the murderer.

"Something wrong?" I asked. "You look like you just got some bad news."

"You feel like dating a newscaster?" she asked meanly. "There's a gay one who's now available."

My stomach crimped. So Helena had broken up with Christine, or vice versa. And it certainly wasn't Christine's newly single status that was on Zena Beth's mind. The fact that Christine was the one she chose to mention — and to me, as if I were some opportunist whose taste in famous lesbian lovers was indiscriminate — was the most painful part.

"Helena just packed up last night, and moved directly into the bedroom of Lila Scott." Lila Scott was once the most in-demand fashion model around; these days she was on the wrong side of forty and a businesswoman handling her own cosmetics line.

"Helena was always like that — she had to have the next lover, the escape hatch, all neatly lined up before she leapt. She never mentioned a word of it to me before. I wonder if Christine knew."

I had no idea how I was supposed to react to all this news, or rather, how I was supposed to react to Zena Beth's reaction. Because the truth was, I could see that she didn't care at all about my opinion of any of it. She was like a drunken bully, bristling for a fight, only the person she wanted to fight with wasn't there — and I was.

I lowered the sound on the television. "I'm already dating the person I want to be dating," I said evenly. "I wish you were, too."

Zena Beth pursed her lips and shook her head slowly, as if I had just said something accurate but in bad taste. She took the remote control and listlessly flipped channels for several minutes, clearly not absorbing anything, just searching for some image that would distract for a moment from her private pain. Then she clicked the set off.

"There was a long stretch in there, when Helena and I were together, when my work was going well, when she was winning events, when we were comfortable and peaceful with each other. I think back on it now, and I realize — *that* was happiness. You always think happiness will arrive with bells on, and you'll feel some sort of perpetual, other-worldly bliss, but you don't. You just feel on course. You don't realize how modest happiness is, that it's just a feeling that it doesn't get better than this.' "

I felt sure that she was only saying these things to me because I was there, because she needed someone to hear, someone to confess to. I knew that nothing more was expected of me than to listen. But

even still, I puzzled over what her message was for
me.

"The worst of it," Zena Beth said, "is that I can't
think of anyone worse for her than Lila Scott."

I thought to ask why, but then I decided I really
didn't care, and Zena Beth was probably wrong,
anyway. "You don't seem to approve of any of
Helena's new lovers," I said instead, trying my best
to sound neutral, to sound as if I thought this was an
acceptable conversation despite the fact that my
insides were leaping and churning in outrage.

"She doesn't realize," Zena Beth said, getting up
to pace, "how finite are the number of people we
can actually love at all in a lifetime. We loved each
other well and long and we should have gone on
together, even if the dynamics between us changed.
We should have lived together into our old age. In all
the great marriages, people end up friends and all the
romantics cluck their tongues in disappointment. How
sad — just friends! But if I get to the end of my days
with even just one close, cherished, never-straying
friend — how rich, how lucky! How absolutely
blessed with luck I'd be."

It was as if the room had opened up between us,
as if some invisible plates in the floor kicked into
action and elongated the distance between us. She
was on stage, the star of one of her plays, and I was
just an undistinguished detail at a far corner. At some
remote center, I thought I heard myself protest —
Look at me! Love me! but then it was gone.

When I went to bed about an hour later — after a
string of little chores meant only to stall my turning
in — Zena Beth was still in the den, pacing. I lay
there listening for a while to the pad of her footsteps

going back and forth, back and forth before I fell
asleep.

By morning, her mood was even blacker, and yet
her confessional urge seemed completely in check.
She moved around the house — making the bed,
putting out breakfast — as if these tasks took
absolutely all her concentration. I didn't try to draw
her into conversation. I showered and packed my bag
and carried it downstairs to the front door. I was
reeling between fury and self-pity.

I sat down at the piano while I waited for the
cab I had called to arrive. One of the Catholic hymns
I had learned during high school was rustily coming
back to me.

"Do I know that song?" Zena Beth said, coming
in to the living room.

"I doubt it," I said, not looking up. "Unless you
used to be in a band with a bunch of nuns."

She sat on the bench next to me. "If you can
stand the company, I thought I'd drive you to the
airport myself."

"I can stand it," I said, feeling a jolt of victory
that she had evidently overheard me arranging for my
own transportation. "We'd better get going, though."

She picked up my bag and carried it out to the
car as I cancelled the cab. Anger was still smoldering
under my skin; she had ruined for us a whole night
and morning of lovemaking. I was annoyed with
myself for marking time this way but it was as if she
had reduced me to my most primal urges.

But it wasn't hormones at all, I knew. I was

dangerously close to being in love. And I was angry at her for ruining even this for me, for making love seem like something desolate and pitiable.

On the open road, the Jaguar was able to work its full magic; I felt as if we were on a flying carpet, sailing with the wind. Zena Beth's mood lifted slightly. She was making an effort at small talk.

"I hope you'll send me some of your other clips," she said. "Not just the interviews you do with me."

"Okay. I'm working on a quirky little story now where I'm trying to calculate the number of cars in Manhattan on a typical day versus how many miles of parkable curb space there is."

"Really?" she said, smiling. "That gives me an idea." She pulled the car off the main highway down a small road that quickly grew shaded with the long shadows of mountains and towering trees. Tendrils of sunlight fell across the road like liquid gold.

"What's this? Some kind of short cut to the airport?"

"More like a detour," she said. "I believe I owe you something."

The wheels of the Jaguar crunched pebbles and twigs as she drove over a small embankment and pulled the car as far into a clearing in the woods as she could without ramming a tree. Then she turned off the engine and glided her seat back as far as it went. She reached over and did the same to mine, looking at me the way she did that first night at the hotel.

"Wait a minute," I said, laughing nervously. "You don't really mean to . . . in broad daylight?"

"Broad daylight in North Carolina woods is not as

broad as it is in Manhattan, my little city slicker," she
said, kissing me.

She caressed my face and neck, more tenderly, I
thought, than she had before, calming my nerves, but
only slightly. What would happen to a person, I
wondered, if a state trooper decided to drive by just
now?

I struggled free. "Look, I really can't relax this
way. For one thing, there's my plane."

She smiled her most seductive smile. "Fresh air
seemed to do something for you yesterday."

She started biting my earlobe and neck,
successfully distracting me from the fact that she had
managed to unzip my jeans. Her hands on my thighs
made me go tingly and weak, and when she gestured
for me to lift up so she could pull my jeans down, I
obliged. I blushed so hotly I broke into a sweat, and
nearly struggled away again, but by then it was too
late. Her fingers were inside me while her thumb
found the place that sent shivers clear down to the
soles of my feet. She hissed nearly inaudible
temptations into my ear, the swirl of her breath
raising goosebumps down my arm. She found a
rhythm that made me grip the back of her neck and
held me there, strung out along the sharply pointed
edges of orgasm. I thought I would sob if she didn't
soon set me free.

And she didn't. She slowed her fingers to a deep,
slow beat, and moved her thumb in a feather-light
pulse that nonetheless hit like tiny shocks. Then
suddenly, she returned to her earlier rhythm,
knocking the wind clear out of me, and leaving me
heaving for breath against the leather seat.

"Better zip up," she said mischievously as she leaned away and pulled the car back onto the road, pointing us back in the direction of the airport.

Even when my breathing returned to normal, I didn't dare ask if she had intended this as reward or retribution.

Nikki had agreed to meet me for dinner Monday night. We had eaten all the way through dessert and I was still talking about Zena Beth.

"I think the worst part is that I don't feel like I'm on any kind of equal footing with her. I mean, I'm back to having to sit by the phone and wait and see if she thinks of me in connection with her weekend plans."

"You're the one who's letting yourself feel that way," Nikki said, pushing her blonde bangs over her forehead with the same hand that held a lit cigarette. "No one said you can't call her and invite her up for the weekend. Just because she's famous, wealthy, gorgeous and older doesn't mean you have to be intimidated."

"Thank you, Ann Landers," I said. "I can just see it now. Zena Beth in my mangy little Ozone Park apartment. I mean, it's bad enough that she is who she is. But then there has to be Helena on top of it. She couldn't have been much clearer about it after this weekend — Helena Zoë is still her life."

"That's okay, tell Zena Beth she can drive me to the airport any time," Nikki said. "In the meantime, if you hate the situation so much, bail out now before you have too much invested and try to get Elaine back."

"Christ, I'm just so tied in knots," I said, resting my head in my hands.

"Well, all I know is you were happy when you were with Elaine, and this doesn't look like happiness to me."

I shut my eyes and remembered the way I always felt on the way to see Elaine — released, lightfooted, hopeful, generous. With Zena Beth, there was an infusion of adrenaline that I recognized as unhealthy — unnatural even. And yet, I was completely hooked.

"I've got to see what happens — what might happen — with Zena Beth."

"Blessed is she with low expectations."

"I thought that was advice only for straight women."

"It's the dirty little secret of lesbian life," Nikki said. "Women can be shits, too."

"Yeah," I said, absent-mindedly patting my mousse with the back of my spoon.

"God, I know it's serious when something chocolate sits in front of you for longer than thirty seconds."

I attempted a smile. I was remembering Zena Beth slicing up the den carpet as she paced back and forth, stewing about Helena. The image was like a small ulcer, something to nurse and finger painfully. The bad moments with her stayed with me longer; casual cruelty always seemed to me to cancel out casual kindness. The latter was easy, and there was usually something in it for the person who was being kind. Cruelty struck me as a more natural state, the person unedited, unabridged. But maybe I was just a cynic. Maybe Zena Beth's true nature was the woman who clung to me in her sleep, who made the shy, nervous phone call to invite me down to visit, who unleashed such hunger when we made love. Maybe.

"Hello in there," Nikki singsonged, waving her hand in front of my face. "Let me have your mousse if you're just going to stare into it like it's a crystal ball. Mousse is made to be eaten."

"You'll regret the calories," I said, sliding the dish over to her side of the table.

"Most things worth doing are worth regretting." She smiled as she slid a spoonful into her mouth.

When I got in from work, I went through my ritual: straight to the tape machine for messages, then sorting through my mail for, in order of desirability, offers from agents to make a movie out of my latest *Hip* article; gossipy letters from far-flung friends, and offers from agents to make a movie out of my gossipy letters to far-flung friends.

There were none of these, but there was a letter, postmarked Madison, Wisconsin, in what I intuitively guessed to be Zena Beth's handwriting. The letter was on hotel stationery, crisply folded; the ink was from a black fountain pen.

> *Dear Joyce:*
> *I'm here at U. of Wisconsin, giving a lecture about theater and radical themes. People never seem to tire of being encouraged to be outrageous. It's a mystery*

to me that more don't want to practice what they're preached.

I'm sorry I behaved badly again during the time we had together this weekend. I don't mean to be so rude but I also don't much see the point in spending time with someone if you have to hide your feelings. Everyone who knows me knows I have strong reactions to anything having to do with H. I don't seem to be able to keep that a secret.

But that's no reflection on you. I sense that you're mature enough to know that. People drag all their leftover lives with them all the time, assaulting newcomers with old anger and disappointment.

You surprise me, and delight me. I'm not always so terrific at saying so. Hope the curb scandal story is a huge success. I'm all for parking, myself.

Zena Beth

I sat down on the bed, pulling off an article of clothing a piece at a time, rereading the letter four times before I had changed into sweats for the night. What did she mean, I surprised her? Was the "delight" reference, in the same paragraph with the parking joke, meant only to refer to our sexual encounters? Was this going to be a pattern in our meetings — that she would hurt me by somehow evoking the memory of Helena, and then apologize sweetly later? "Sorrys" eventually lose their power to heal or even soothe. What did she want from me, anyway?

What *did* she want — it was the only question that really mattered. Because I knew what I wanted. And she hadn't even signed off the letter with "love."

I was on my third draft of a letter responding to Zena Beth when the phone rang. I stepped over the crumpled and discarded drafts on the floor to answer.

"Am I speaking with Joyce Ecco?" the confident and pleasant female voice asked.

"Yes, who is this?"

"Oh, Joyce, hello! This is Lucinda Blackmun, a friend of Zena Beth's. But call me Luce, please — everyone else does and Zena Beth says I completely deserve it."

I laughed, my initial wariness having almost completely dissipated. There was something appealingly intimate about a friend of Zena Beth's — one she had never mentioned to me by name — knowing enough about me to be calling.

"Zena Beth's away right now," Luce said, starting to answer my unasked question, "but I usually come by to look after the horses — just the emotional stuff. She's got a stable girl for the real work. And the cook and the housekeeper are in and out, too — which explains why I'm in Zena Beth's kitchen right now, using her phone and her phone book. So I can invite you to the surprise party I'm throwing for her birthday."

"Oh, really — I had no idea. That it was her birthday, I mean."

"No, you wouldn't. Few people would. It

probably comes as a surprise to many people — even
those few close to her — that Zena Beth even has a
birthday at all. She has this way of giving the
impression that she's above a lot of the commonplace
joys and pains the rest of us experience." She
laughed. "I mean that kindly, of course. It's one of
her assets, and probably how she got as far as she
has. I should know — we go back twenty years. The
point I'm trying to make is that those of us who are
her friends have to go around reminding her she's a
mere mortal and would like things like a birthday
party."

I glanced at Zena Beth's letter, its graceful
handwritten message nearly committed to memory
now. "Well, I'm flattered that you're inviting me."
What did Zena Beth tell her about me, I was dying
to ask but wouldn't dare. "When is it?"

"Well, that's the slightly complicated part. The
bad news is that it's short notice — this Saturday
night. But the good news is that it's in your neck of
the woods — at the 21 Club. See, the party's been
set for months now, but since you're a recent arrival
on the scene, I was forced to call you late. Can you
make it?"

Goosebumps rose on my arms as I imagined being
just one of dozens of Zena Beth's young female
distractions at the party. Nightmarish visions danced
in my head. "Um, who else will be there?"

"I'm having it in New York so she can fulfill all
her obligations to people in the theater and book
world — producers, agents, editors, some key actors
— people she needs to schmooze with. Then there
are assorted old friends, such as myself. Helena and
her latest, of course. A few other old lovers who

haven't fallen out of favor. Some hopelessly devoted students and groupies of various origins, some too embarrassing to mention, who would impale themselves on sharpened dildos if they weren't invited. And you."

I wasn't crazy about the reference to me in proximity to groupies and dildos, but I chose not to dwell on it. "Well, sure, I guess so — I mean, I'd love to. But God, I have nothing to wear, and what does a person give Zena Beth Frazer for her fortieth birthday?"

"So you did know this was the big four-oh."

"Yes, but not because she mentioned it."

"Very little that you learn about Zena Beth will be because she told you."

I could hear Luce smiling. I had a feeling I could trust her, that she was going to be valuable to me. "Do you really think she'll be surprised?"

"Oh, yes, no problem. I told her I'm taking her to 21's for a birthday dinner. It works out nicely because she's away and needs to fly back to the east coast on her way back from this Wisconsin thing. I just neglected to mention that a hundred other people would be joining us."

"A hundred people?"

"Don't you worry about a thing. The outfit or the gift. As little of both is the order of the day. Make sure you find me at the party. See you about eight, then? I'll be ushering in Zena Beth about eight-thirty, so don't be late."

— 8 —

The 21 Club was just the sort of place I could see Zena Beth liking. Nothing overtly lavish about it, yet understated good taste and style hummed in every discreet detail. A tuxedoed man directed me up to the private room where the party was being held, and I saw with immense relief that the paneled room was already comfortably full. I headed straight for the bar, ordered a gin and tonic, and tried my best to hide behind it.

I sat on a black leather bar stool and put on my reporter face, my best I'm-not-participating-I'm-just-here-to-catch-you-in-the-act face. I scanned the room for Helena and Lila without success. Neither of them would be easy to miss, so I assumed they hadn't arrived yet.

While pretending to be fascinated with my ice cubes, I glanced quickly around and decided that I had chosen the right thing to wear. I had Nikki to thank for that. She had insisted on going shopping with me and had chosen this simple (she called it classic) black dress that I figured cost more alone than the sum total of my entire current winter wardrobe. But Nikki, being a far more loyal reader of fashion magazines than I was, assured me that black was very New York and very serviceable and I would be able to accessorize the dress into oblivion for decades, making it well worth its price tag.

Meanwhile, I was left to contemplate my feet — which were reasonably comfortable in the pumps that had been our compromise choice. I had been favoring the Red Cross version and Nikki had been partial to a pair that seemed to have been designed for a woman with two toes per foot. We had had a brief spat over the fact that I considered her fashion tastes politically incorrect. She won, and as a result I had on a full arsenal of makeup and jewelry and had blow-dried my hair and dabbed perfume until I felt worthy of a place like this. But I couldn't help feeling just a little bit queasy, a little bit like I was in drag. I held my clutch pocketbook like a football; the appeal of such an item had always eluded me. There was nothing as ergonomically well-designed as the back pocket of a pair of jeans.

When I was reasonably confident that I had melted into the background, I allowed myself to swivel around slowly and more fully take in the room. Two long, elegantly prepared tables boasted every manner of decadent hors d'oeuvres — caviar, Camembert, lobster tails, shrimp, sliced Nova Scotia salmon, liver pâté, and a host of pale, exotic-looking vegetables.

There were only slightly more women in the room than men and everyone looked comfortably chic in dinner jackets and tuxes (his and hers). It was a loud, lively crowd, many of whom seemed to know each other, and none of whom, thankfully, seemed to know me. On the other hand, none of them were making an effort to, either. Maybe the dress was all wrong, after all. My back went clammy.

But there was no time to wonder — all attention had turned to the doorway, where Zena Beth and another woman had suddenly appeared. Zena Beth let out a little gasp — I heard it distinctly though I was at the far end of the room — and then everyone exploded into cheers and applause and shouts of "Happy Birthday!" and "Congratulations!"

The crowd descended on her so quickly, offering kisses and hugs, that I didn't see more than a glimpse of her for the next hour. When I did, she was weaving her way through the throng, working the room like a politician in the last weeks of a campaign. She had on a silky bronze pantsuit that clung slightly and occasionally to her hips and breasts, and rippled regally at the sleeves and legs. I worked hard not to stare after her, but it was nearly hopeless. It was as if every molecule of me cried out for her.

When I saw that she and the woman she had arrived with were finally heading my way, my heart

began to pound. It was as if I were meeting her
again for the first time. The setting, the occasion,
seemed to erase the tenuous hold I thought I might
have had on her. And it seemed for a second that
she did not know me, either. Her eyes met mine just
a few feet away with not a flash of familiarity. But
then, recognition — and there was no mistaking it,
joy — washed over her face.

"Joyce," she said, taking hold of my hands, "how
did you —" She turned and looked at the boyish,
wild-haired woman next to her. "Luce, is this the
mark of your matchmaking ways?"

Luce smiled enigmatically and winked at me.
"Wasn't me who made the match," she said. "Nice
to meet you in person, Joyce."

Zena Beth turned back to scrutinize me. Then she
leaned forward and whispered, "My God, you were
pretty before, but now you've gotten beautiful."

I was reckless, over the edge with wanting her.
But I didn't have a chance to respond. There was
another commotion at the door.

"Must be Lila and Helena," Luce said. The crowd
parted slightly and two tall, slim women began to
weave their way toward us.

Lila Scott was instantly recognizable. She was
easily the most photographed face in the room.
Diamond teardrop earrings glittered through her
blonde, shoulder-length hair, an accent to her silver,
forties-style cocktail dress. And though she was
beautiful, all eyes shifted swiftly to Helena, who, with
her sleek, shorn, white-blonde hair and purposeful
stride, effortlessly commanded attention. As she got
closer, Lila slipped her hand through Helena's arm.

"Happy birthday, darling," Helena said, unhesitatingly kissing Zena Beth on the lips.

It registered with me like a brisk slap, and I sat stunned while the noisy greetings went on all around me. Zena Beth had shifted her body forward almost imperceptibly; how neatly they seemed to fit next to each other.

"Helena, this is Joyce Ecco," Zena Beth said.

Helena reached forward and pressed my hand with her own broad, cool palm. "Pleased to meet you," she said.

"I feel we already have," I said, and the four of them exploded in laughter. A deep blush traveled up Helena's neck to her cheeks; I felt myself match it. How much, exactly, had Zena Beth confided to them all?

Zena Beth, one hand on each of their backs, led Lila and Helena to the hors d'oeuvres table like a good hostess. I stared after them, nearly limp with jealousy.

"Very nice comeback to an awfully awkward moment," Luce said. She ordered a drink.

"I didn't mean it as a dig. It was just the truth, and it just popped out."

"She's told you a lot about Helena?" Luce said, pulling up a stool.

"Well, she talks about her a lot. That's told me more than anything." My stomach clenched in fear as soon as the comment was out. Who was I to be criticizing Zena Beth Frazer to the woman who was very likely her best friend?

"Very astute of you, Ms. Ecco," Luce said. She gave me a lingering smile full of warm reassurance.

"Come on," she said, taking a swig of her drink. "Let's go for a walk around the block. Come on," she coaxed, sensing my reluctance.

We walked up the steps to the street which was lined with turn-of-the-century brownstones. Luce gave me her blazer when she saw me shiver.

"Zena Beth and I were lovers once, briefly, a hundred years ago," Luce said as we started to stroll. "We make much better friends, so no regrets. But I remember how hard she was. I think she's even harder now. I'd just hate to see someone as nice as you take it personally."

I made fists in the blazer's pocket and let her comment settle.

"All I mean is it's not going to be easy. Remember how many people over the years were grabbing at a piece of Zena Beth Frazer, the institution, the mythological goddess. And Helena's leaving her — it took her down to the bottom of the well."

I didn't trust myself to say more about Zena Beth, not now, not to Luce, who knew too much. "What about you? Are you here with someone?"

"Me? No. I'm single at the moment. Of course, 'moment' is a relative term. In this case it's lasted two years."

When Luce laughed, her eyes crinkled and long dimples pressed into her cheeks. With her salt-and-pepper hair, spiky and slightly punk, and firm, olive skin, I imagined plenty of women found her attractive.

"I hope I didn't inspire you to feel sorry for me," she said, touching my elbow protectively as we crossed against the light. "For a long time I was

afraid of slamming doors on relationships — bad
relationships — just because something was an affront
to my pride. But then I realized my pride was
important and it's not a failure to end a lousy
relationship."

I nodded solemnly, feeling dwarfed by the years
of experience, and likely pain, that went into her
revelation. I thought it better to change the subject.
"You must be a fan of Mountville, too."

"I am. It's a place you either love or hate. And
it's been good to me. I'm a potter and there aren't a
lot of places left in the country where you can
actually make a living that way. My expenses are low
enough that I live comfortably, and I sell enough in
town and during traveling shows that I don't starve."

"I used to love to go to crafts fairs." Actually, it
was Elaine who loved to go and taught me to love
them. "Maybe I own a Blackmun and I don't even
realize it."

"Well, I'd be flattered. Come on, we should be
getting back," Luce said. "It's an amazing group of
people who are assembled. I really ought to let you
socialize."

The room had heated up and grown several
decibel levels louder by the time we returned. Luce
quickly got drawn into boisterous conversation with a
group of women and all the bar stools were taken.
Zena Beth and Helena were nowhere in sight.

Pushing my way to the bar, I got another drink. I
wasn't a big drinker, but tonight I felt an urge to get
spectacularly drunk.

I leaned against a wall, rigid with
self-consciousness. This was exactly what I'd most
feared, why I'd nearly backed out. Only Nikki's shrill

insistence had shamed me into coming. And what for? Zena Beth obviously preferred to spend the evening with Helena, even if Helena was with someone else.

Just then, two tuxedoed men burst through the swinging doors carrying a flaming cake, their rich tenors leading everyone in a spirited version of "Happy Birthday." Applause filled the room as the cake was placed on a table in front of Zena Beth, who seemed to be drawing herself up the way she did before one of her lectures.

"I really — I find myself nearly speechless," she said, "and you know how unusual that is." The room guffawed in unison.

Watching her, I felt my anger drain away. Her sleek good looks still hit me hard. She was both everything I wanted to be and everything I wanted to have. I saw her above me in bed, kissing me. Even if only some of what she might feel for me was real, it would be worth it.

"It's incredible to have so many of the people closest to me here tonight, people who've known me back in the days when I couldn't have gotten a job in the kitchen at a place like this, let alone be hosted at it. A special toast first and foremost to Luce — where are you, Luce?" Zena Beth asked, raising her champagne glass — "for always knowing what's best for me, even when I don't."

She reeled off next a string of names I didn't recognize, though I had a feeling they were various business associates.

"And of course, Helena. Thanks for flying in, especially considering that it cuts into ski season."

She caught Helena's eye across the room, and it

was as if every muscle in her body strained forward. I couldn't tell whether anyone else noticed, but it hit me swiftly and sharply, like ice on the exposed nerve of a tooth.

I knew not to expect it, as surely as I knew anything ever in my life, and yet I was absolutely leveled when she ended her comments, urging the crowd to keep eating and partying, without directing a word at me. I immediately tried to reassure myself. It was only my vanity that wanted some public recognition of our coupledom. The only thing that really mattered was that she made time for me in private.

I drained my drink and as I lowered the glass, I found myself face to face with Zena Beth. No one was trailing her. We were alone — as much as we could be in such a crowd — for the first time all night.

"Excuse me, Madam, but are you here with anyone?"

"Well, if I were," I teased back, "your question would put me in a compromising position."

"If I have my way, I'll be putting you in several compromising positions."

We both laughed, and headed outside to hail a cab.

I woke to hear Zena Beth ordering breakfast, room service. The sound of her voice, her light, lilting accent, soothed the rough edges of waking. It was a voice, it occurred to me while still in the subterranean innocence of near-sleep, that I could

wake up to the rest of my life. "Good morning,
birthday girl," I said.

She smiled like a child recalling all the candles
she had blown out in one breath. "Thank you for my
wonderful bookmark," she said, fingering it. I had
gone back to Tiffany's and gotten her the sterling
silver triangle bookmark engraved with her initials. "It
was a grand bash, wasn't it? Did you enjoy yourself?"
she asked.

"The post-party activities were my personal
favorite, if you must know," I said, pulling the sheet
up around my shoulders for warmth.

"Child, you could raise the dead."

"I have my hands full with the living, thank you."

"You're in fine spirits," she said, tracing a line
over the sheet, down my stomach and hips.

"And why not? We're here, together."

When she took her hand away and straightened
up, I realized my mistake. I forgot, in the languidness
of the moment, that we weren't in love. We were
lovers, but we weren't in love. "Let me run to the
bathroom," I mumbled.

Over the water in the sink, I heard the rattle of
dishes and the conversation of the bellhop wheeling
in our breakfast. I pulled the bulky terry cloth robe
tightly around me as I sat down across from her at
the small round table. Sun glinted off the silver
serving platters.

"It'll be summer before you know it," Zena Beth
said, spreading jam on a bagel. "I love the way
Mountville looks in the summer. I just have to live
close to the earth. I love New York, Joyce, but I
could never live here."

I struggled to keep my face a mask, but I knew

my disappointment was showing. I rubbed my eyes to fight off a scowl.

"Do you ever think you could live somewhere else?" she asked.

"This is all I've ever known. It's home to me, the way some small town is home to a lot of the rest of America. New York is my little town, I guess." I swallowed a forkful of scrambled eggs, realizing all at once that my stomach was burning with hunger. I had barely eaten a bite last night. "I mean, I'm interested in other areas," I added hastily, not wanting to insult her, not wanting to ward off an invitation to visit her again. "Almost everywhere else is more beautiful than New York, that's for sure. My parents love Arizona now that they're out there, and I never thought they'd leave Queens. It just never occurred to me to actually live somewhere else. Everything I wanted was always here."

"Is it now?"

My legs went weak and what felt like a spring uncoiled in my stomach. I knew now to be suspicious of her questions. Anything might be used against me later. "I'm not sure what you mean," I said slowly.

She put her fork down. "This isn't my strong suit, darlin'," she said, reaching across the linen tablecloth to hook a finger through two of mine. "Are you going to make me spell it out?"

My face was tight and hot. "I honestly don't know what you mean . . . but you're scaring me."

She was. I felt like I was in the lead car of a rollercoaster, stalled at the top of its tallest hill.

She leaned back in her chair. "I really don't have any right to ask. I'm not offering you anything conventional, certainly not anything particularly convenient." She got up and paced. "There aren't a lot of jobs — jobs that make careers, I mean — down in Mountville, the way you'll find up here. There's no *Hip,* for instance. No nonstop nightlife or Broadway or . . . whatever it is that you love here. I'm embarrassed to see that I haven't bothered to find out a whole lot about what you love. Except that —"

She went over to the window where the glare bleached away the expression on her face. "Except that I've let myself believe you care about me. And I know I'd rather have you in Mountville, with me, than a couple of hundred miles away. But I don't know if that's enough for you. I do know that it's a lot to ask."

I was frozen in my seat. Even if I'd known what it was I wanted to say, I doubted my vocal chords would have cooperated. Wasn't this the fantasy, so cherished that I hadn't even allowed myself to imagine it?

"Of course I don't expect you to answer me now, this minute, this week, even. You've got a hundred little things to consider. There's plenty of room in the house for both of us, though, and I'll do everything I can to help you look for work. But you don't have to worry about money. Whatever you earned would be your own. I certainly wouldn't expect you to help support the house . . . in fact, I'd insist that you didn't. I work a lot, I travel a lot. I think you know that. You'd be welcome to join me in some of the traveling if that interested you. People in Mountville know about me, if that's a concern, but no one has ever bothered me. I go to town meetings like everyone else and have my say. Otherwise, it's a beautiful place and ..."

She came back over and sat down stiffly at the table. "Well, that's all I can think of."

It's a beautiful place and ... *what*? It's a beautiful place and we'd be together. It's a beautiful place and I love you. I waited, but nothing more seemed to occur to her. A lump in my throat made it hard for me to speak, and my eyes were stinging.

"Joyce, what is it? If you think it's a terrible idea, please say so now."

"No, I ... it's just not ... Don't people say other things to each other first?" My cheeks were steaming. I couldn't look up. "I really — I really have no idea how you feel about me." To my horror, a hot, sluggish tear lumbered from the corner of my eye.

She came over and squatted by my chair. "Don't you know," she whispered, "that I'm just as scared as you are?" She took my hand. "I don't know if I can say all the things people say. I don't know if I can *feel* all the things people feel anymore. Don't think I'm cruel. I just want you to know what you're getting into."

Nobody ever knows what she's getting into, I told myself. If we did, no one would ever fall in love.

− 9 −

I'll have dessert only if you split it with me," Caryn was telling Nikki. The two of them huddled behind one menu across the table from me. Nikki had chosen one of her favorite spots in Soho for the occasion of my meeting the woman from work she had gotten delusional over.

For one thing, Nikki was convinced Caryn was about to forsake heterosexual life for her. But just because a straight woman flirted didn't prove a thing. I was rehearsing these reprimands in my mind, waiting for my chance to get Nikki alone, when

Caryn excused herself to go to the bathroom. Nikki watched her until she was sure she was safely sequestered.

"So, is she hot, or what? Don't you think she's funny? You gotta admit she's funny. So, come on, tell me what you think before she gets back. Do you like her?"

"Nikki," I said, massaging my temples. "Get yourself out of this now, before it's too late."

Nikki pushed back hard against the booth. Her blue eyes narrowed. "Great. That's just great. Thanks for the insight."

"Nik, you know I'm thinking of you here. The woman is getting some kind of private kick out of getting you going. I'm sure it makes her feel good. But even if she's conscious of what's going on, she isn't going to do anything about it —"

"You're wrong there. We already slept together. Last night."

I stared dumbly. Nikki crossed her arms. "I was going to tell you. But there was no time. And she doesn't want anyone to know, so it was just as well that you didn't have to pretend the whole meal."

"Well, for God's sake, don't hold out on me now, Nikki. What happened?" I glanced over my shoulder. "There's time. Straight girls take forever in the john."

Nikki pursed her lips primly. "It's not funny anymore — the straight girl jokes."

"Good God. You're not in love with her, are you?"

"You know, she could just be coming out. This could be her time. It doesn't have to be a straight girl window-shopping."

"No, but you've got a track record, old buddy. All the way back to high school and Monica DiMaria."

"Please, don't remind me." Nikki sagged in her seat and lit a fresh cigarette. "But I think you're right about this part. I think I am in love. It's ridiculous and a pain in the ass. We work together and she's got a fiancé. But there it is."

"Does *he* have any idea?"

"Are you crazy? Shhhh, here she comes. Hey, you know who I saw out the other night at Skinny's? Elaine."

My body went rigid. I barely glanced at Caryn as she sat back down at the table, her curly hair freshly fluffed, her lips newly lipsticked. "Who was she with?"

"Pat and Susan. I only spotted them as they were leaving. I only saw them for a second."

Pat and Susan were a couple we had considered our best friends, a couple we went out with often, confided our little fights and simple pleasures to. So they had chosen sides. I hadn't heard from any of our old friends since the breakup. But what did I expect? I had left Elaine, after all. I was in a new relationship, wasn't I? Elaine deserved all our friends. She was the one who had earned their loyalty and trust.

"I'm sorry. Am I interrupting?" Caryn said. "Want me to go away again?"

"No," Nikki and I said simultaneously. I stirred the ice in my empty glass so hard a small shard flew out.

"No, it's okay. I just said something stupid," Nikki said. "Raising the dead, you could say."

"Jesus, don't use that expression," I said.

"Hey, sorry. Private joke, I guess," Nikki said to Caryn.

Out on the street, we all shuffled pointlessly, waiting for someone else to decide how to spend the rest of the evening. I resisted the pressure to excuse myself, now that I knew Nikki and Caryn were a couple, however odd and tentative. But I couldn't do it. I needed to talk to Nikki alone. And Nikki seemed to know it.

"Hey, Caryn, let me help you get a cab. We've all got work tomorrow," Nikki said. She walked Caryn, in her pointy-toed heels, to the curb, while she tried to flag a taxi.

I watched them laughing easily together, occasionally touching each other's arm, and wondered whether Nikki might be right. Maybe Caryn wouldn't go back. Maybe she wouldn't get scared. Maybe Nikki wouldn't get burned this time.

Nikki held the cab's door open and Caryn slid in. I saw Caryn's fingers touch the back of Nikki's head while they kissed goodbye.

Nikki came back over, lipstick smeared on her upper lip, and grinning broadly.

"Okay, okay, she's hot," I said. "And she seems bright . . . and sweet. But don't say I didn't warn you."

"Thanks, coach," she said, tossing an arm around my shoulder. "Now, no more private jokes. What's on your mind?" She steered us over to a parked car and we leaned against its cold steel body.

"How'd she look? Elaine. Did she look good?"

"Yeah, she looked good. She looked the same."

Nikki was frowning, concerned. I couldn't tell her, couldn't explain. I just wasn't ready to think of Elaine as part of my past. The only way I'd been able to cope with it was not to think of her at all. And when I was with Zena Beth, that was possible. Being with Zena Beth was like being in a total eclipse.

"She asked me to go down to North Carolina and live with her."

"*What!* Are you *kidding* me? You're kidding me — to get back at me for the bombshell about me and Caryn. Aren't you?" I shook my head. "Holy shit. Joyce, this is like . . . this is like winning the Lesbian Lotto or something," she exclaimed, clapping my shoulders hard. "You must be wild with excitement. My God, you're a celebrity! I'm standing next to a goddamn celebrity." Nikki was infectious, and I allowed myself to feel a little of the thrill I'd been warding off. "So why do you look like you just ate your last meal?"

"It's a lot, Nik. I'd have to quit my job. My parents are no problem — and they'll probably be thrilled I'm moving somewhere more sane and safe than New York. But you know, I've lived here forever. I don't know if I'll like it down South."

"From the way you say the two of you carry on all the time, you probably won't see much of it anyway."

"Let's walk. My butt is freezing." I ground my fists into the pockets of my coat and shivered. "That's what I'm afraid of, Nikki. What am I? Just her live-in sexual relief? Someone to keep her off the streets?"

"Whoa, where's this coming from?"

"I don't know if she has a heart, Nikki. It's not like it sounds. It's not like she says she loves me." I wiped away a film of tears.

"Look, Joyce, I'm not there with you when the two of you are together. I don't know her at all. Maybe you don't, either. But I do know you. And I know you like to see things through, that you're an all-or-nothing kind of person. If you say no to this, what then? You'll torture yourself every time she's not up here, or you're not down there, wondering what she's up to. And if it fizzles out, you'll tell yourself it was your fault because you didn't give it a hundred percent. And look, if you're thinking of Elaine" — I jumped at the mention of her name — "it's over, Joyce. It's not going to be any more over if you leave town."

I whirled around and grabbed Nikki by the lapel of her coat. "Was she with someone? She was with someone the night you saw her and you're not telling me, right?"

"Will it make you feel better or worse, Joyce?"

"I just want the truth."

"No — you don't." She pried my hand free of her coat. "You just want everything unchanged. Well, welcome to life."

Nikki hailed a cab at the next corner. I told her I wanted to walk a few more blocks in the cold, and I did. I had to try to imagine my life without Nikki a subway ride away, without this city I'd been born in and lived in my whole life, without, finally, Elaine. Because that's what it came down to: this choice, this having to forsake one woman for another. Even though Elaine and I had been apart, just sensing her nearby, knowing that we might be crossing paths, that she might be an arm's length away, was a small comfort, even if it was an illusion. Now the prospect of distance loomed like an abyss.

I switched to more practical worries. Of course I'd work. I'd get a job at whatever was the biggest paper in town. Some two-bit paper I'd end up running inside of a year, I humored myself. And then, if I came back home, that would look great on the resumé, that would bump me up a few rungs on the ladder, wouldn't it?

And maybe I'd end up liking it, even. It *was* beautiful. People lived perfectly productive and meaningful lives outside of New York City. Certainly more peaceful and healthy lives.

And then there was Zena Beth herself. I hadn't really let myself think of her at all. I couldn't. It was an unfair advantage. It was like a ton of bricks on that side of the scale.

Without being conscious of making a decision, I realized the problem had shifted, as if between footfalls, from whether I'd move to Mountville, to how and when I'd get there. And how I'd tell Elaine. Because that was one thing I knew for sure: I had to tell Elaine myself.

When I shut the door behind me in W.B. Dyer's office, I felt the resolve drain from my body like air out of a slit tire. The top halves of his office walls were glass, so it didn't feel as though we were in a private space, but I had never been in such close quarters with my boss before. He always gave me his spare and monotone directions out in the noisy, bustling newsroom. It had been enough of a buffer to keep intimidation at bay.

He was nearly as famous as some of the people we covered, but he never carried himself that way. He had been at *Life* and *Look,* he had written a book about Vietnam that was made into a movie, and he was now part owner of *Hip,* as well as being its managing editor. I had had to make an appointment to get even these five minutes, and when I sank into the steel chair across from his steel desk, I was conscious of time ticking away.

"Mr. Dyer, thanks for seeing me."

He looked up briefly from the manuscript he was editing on his lap and shrugged. "Why shouldn't I? You work here, don't you?"

"I, uh, well that's kind of what this is about."

"Ah, you got a better job." He put his pencil down. "I'm not surprised. You have a lot of talent, Ecco."

My throat went painfully dry. "Well, yes, that's it," I lied. "But the thing is, it's out of state. In North Carolina, actually."

His eyebrows scaled his forehead and stayed there. "Oh?"

"It's quite a step up for me. I'll be city desk editor," I lied some more.

He bounced his pencil on the steel desk a few times. "Yes. Well, I know a lot of people recommend that route to young people. Be a big fish in a small pond first."

He didn't have to say it, but I knew he thought such advice — if it meant leaving Manhattan — insane. I didn't even want to think about what he would have said if he knew I was leaving without a job at all.

"I guess I wanted to say what a great experience it's been working with you, and *Hip*."

He frowned. "You can still change your mind, Ecco. I'm sure I can't match the salary of a city desk editor — particularly if you're spending it in North Carolina — but I can maybe see if I can get you a little raise, if that would make you reconsider."

"That's incredibly generous. I'm stunned, really. I'm so flattered —"

"This isn't the prom, Ecco. You're a good reporter, that's all. Do you want to work here?"

I cautioned myself not to get emotional. "I do. But this is a good opportunity, too, Mr. Dyer. And . . . and . . ." I felt the need to explain myself, to make it clear that my hand was forced slightly, that *Hip* was superior, should I ever need to come back. "And there is a relationship involved, actually."

"Oh." He leaned back in his chair and poised his pencil over his manuscript again. "That." He smiled at me, but it wasn't the same smile he'd occasionally given me when he liked my copy. "Good luck to you, then."

I felt my cheeks go hot and puffy with shame. *I'm not following a man,* I wanted to shout at him across the desk. *It's not the same thing.* But he had already looked away. And when I opened his office door to leave, I wondered if maybe it was.

Dear Joyce:
This letter finds me in Santa Fe. It's easy to see why Georgia O. loved it out here. Such

a place of extreme and dramatic colors and landscape. But I do love Mountville best. I hope you'll grow to love it, too.

I'm not going to worry about you, if you say not to. You're mature beyond your years. I think I knew that from our first meeting. But I was, too, at your age, and I know sometimes that's just stubbornness masquerading as resolve. You can change your mind. I want you to want to come.

I don't mean to be so stingy. Hard-hearted. Luce says sometimes I'm just a boulder with legs. Maybe that's too harsh even for me. But I'm not a songbird, I know that. I don't sing love songs. But I have my instincts. I always fly home. Especially now that I know that's where you'll be.

Love,
Zena Beth

As I turned down Elaine's block, the sun broke through the thin film of gray clouds. It cheered me and made me hopeful, though about what I wasn't sure. I wasn't going to ask for a reconciliation. It was too late for that, I chastened myself, ticking off all the details that were in place now. I was half packed. The moving company was booked. The landlord was showing my apartment. My resumé was in the mail to the two local papers within driving distance of Mountville. Zena Beth was even having "my" room freshly painted.

I went down the few steps of Elaine's brownstone

and rang the bell. My heart was pounding hard; I hadn't stood here in two months, since the last time we'd made love. Everything felt as familiar as yesterday, as familiar as my own, and yet it was as if another plane of time had sealed itself around this door, these steps, freezing it in place, shutting me out.

I pressed the bell again, and tried to look in the living room window. The blinds were closed tight, but I imagined I could see in, anyway. The maroon couch, all her black and white prints standing around like oversized playing cards, and the bedroom, with its fluffy down quilt, beyond that. And the ghosts of all our days and nights together: dressed up to leave for a dinner out, falling into bed laughing, curled up on the couch talking or harmonizing to some new song on the radio we discovered we both loved. Happiness, on tiny cat feet, walked silently around inside, out of my reach.

Even though it was clear she wasn't home, I kept ringing the bell as if I could will her to materialize. And what for? What did I want from her, she could rightly and angrily ask. I sat down on the cold cement steps, unable to leave.

Oh, Elaine. A strange thing has happened. This strange other woman has happened to me. Can you forgive me? Can you believe me when I say that the best part of me remains, stays behind, here, with you? Elaine. Why couldn't you save me from myself?

I pulled the folded piece of paper from my back pocket that I had carried here just in case. I tried not to think of where she might be, or with whom. "If you need me," was all I had written, with the Mountville address. It was arrogant, maybe she'd even think it was cruel. But somehow I needed to keep a tie to her, even if it was just this thin, tangled cord, stretched perhaps to its breaking, across the hundreds of miles I was about to put between us.

— 10 —

A dull ache spanned my shoulder blades. I lay in bed, flat on my back, praying that I wouldn't have a spasm.

"I told you not to try to unpack a lifetime all in one day, honey." Zena Beth came into the room, carrying a steaming cup, and put it on the table next to my side of the bed.

"I'm sorry. I guess I'm not going to be much fun tonight." I struggled to an upright position and took a sip of tea.

"That's okay. There's no hurry now."

"Does that mean behind the wheel in the woods is not a favored position?"

Smiling, she put on a pair of small, wire-rimmed glasses I'd never seen before. Then she pulled a thick manuscript off her night table and propped it on her upright knees.

"What's that?"

"A book a friend wrote. I promised to give it a blurb."

"Oh." I shut my eyes and pretended to relax, but relaxation was the farthest thing from my mind. There were still whole chunks of her life I knew nothing about, friends I'd never heard of, plans I wasn't part of. In the past when I'd imagined myself finally living with a woman, I thought I would know every last thing about her, that the life we had would be ours together, equally made and worried over. Instead, I felt like a perpetual outsider, a mere visitor in what was now supposed to be my home, too.

"Is this light bothering you?" she asked.

"No."

"Honey, if something is bothering you, you should tell me. Because I can't always guess. Some people are good at that, but you should know I'm not one of them."

I made a fist under the sheets. Lesson one: "Honey" was a term of endearment to be dreaded and despised. And if she told me one more time that she was to be pardoned for being emotionally handicapped, I was going to scream.

"My back is killing me, that's all."

"Come. Turn over. I give a good massage."

She didn't lie. Her hands seemed to know exactly where the pain was crouching, and the pressure was enough to loosen the tension without making me wince. Plus she was untiring. I finally had to tell her enough.

"God, where'd you learn that?" I mumbled into the mattress.

"The horses. I took a course with a vet. It's very important that they have their muscles worked over regularly. If they get sore, they can't rub it themselves."

"I suppose I'd better learn to ride, huh?"

"You might do better learning how to drive first. It's more practical for going to the supermarket, not to mention work."

I rolled over and saw that she was grinning at me. "I happen to already have a driver's license," I said with mock indignation.

"If you're like most New Yorkers, you've used it every other summer weekend to drive out to Fire Island. Which, I hate to be the one to break the news, rates you somewhere beneath a Sunday driver."

"Well, there aren't too many things to hit out here, anyway, from what I can tell," I jibed back. "A muskrat here, a spotted squirrel there."

She smiled, adjusted her glasses, and returned her attention to the manuscript.

Panic clawed at my stomach. A car. I hadn't even thought about that. How in hell was I going to get around? How much did a rusted-out bomb cost down here, I wondered. I'd have to get a paper tomorrow and check out some ads.

But right now, I didn't want to think any more about the problems my being here had created. I leaned over and ran my finger along the underside of her thigh.

"I thought you were out of commission," she said.

"I've had a miraculous recovery."

"An act of God, I'm sure." She put her manuscript aside. "You're like a kitten with a new ball of yarn. Can't settle down."

"Settle down. An interesting choice of words. Is that what we're doing?"

"You tell me."

"Why don't you tell me? For a change." I leaned over and kissed her eyelid to distract from the anger I was afraid had crept into my voice.

She pushed me onto my back again and kissed my throat. She was right — there was no hurry. We made love slowly, deliberately, like sightseers on a riverboat cruise. I felt flushed with knowing her body better and better, feeling it warm and mold under my hands like clay. And as always she whispered to me from some deep and private place, a voice shaded with need and awe, a voice I never heard outside of bed, when her head, not her body, ruled.

When we had tired ourselves out, she lay with her cheek against my shoulder. Even with the lights out, the bedroom wasn't dark. The country night sky, which I had always thought so black, seemed alive with stars and moonlight.

"I have a trip next week. Louisville," she said sleepily.

"Already?"

"There's an experimental theater there. They want me to hear a read-through on a play. It'll be a few days."

"I need to look for a job, right away."

It was what I thought she'd want me to do. But
inside, I felt slashed, scalded, betrayed. What
difference did it make where I was — here or in New
York — if I was going to be without her? She was
still just dropping in.

"You'll write me letters?" I asked.

"One a day if you like."

I kissed the top of her head. "I like." I wanted
her letters. In her letters, at least, she had started to
sign "love."

I woke myself up, yelling. I was sitting bolt
upright in bed, straining into the dark. The yell had
been baritone, an outrage, as if I had been kicked in
the ribs.

"It's okay." Zena Beth was whispering, pressing
my shoulder. Her voice startled me. I hadn't known
where I was, except that I didn't belong.

Slowly, the confusion lifted. I felt my muscles
uncoil and I lay back down. The room was still dark
gray, colorless, but I recognized it.

"I uh, don't usually do that," I said, awake
enough now to be embarrassed. The truth was, I had
never done it before.

"You were fighting to get at someone or
something," she said, curling against my back.

I held her hand against my breast. "I can't
remember," I said. And I didn't try. I didn't really
want to know.

* * * * *

"But it's ridiculous. I can't accept this." We were standing in front of a copper Saab parked in the driveway. She had hurried me through breakfast without saying why, and then when she walked me to the car, told me it was mine.

"It isn't ridiculous. It makes sense to have a second car around. Think of it that way if it helps." She had on a plaid lumberjacket and muddy boots up to her knees.

"I was going to buy my own car. Something I could afford to pay off. I can't pay off a brand new Saab."

"No one's asking you to," she said. "It's a gift."

"A gift like this isn't a gift. It's a burden."

"I'm sorry you feel that way," she said. "But I think it's pretty silly. I have more money than you do, and will for a while. I'm not going to respect you more if you drive around in a car that's taped together and hacks like my Great Aunt Coozie."

"Your Great Aunt *who*?" I said, trying my best not to be jollied out of my protest.

"Look, if it makes you feel better, it's not yours," Zena Beth said. "It's mine, and it's on permanent loan to you. I know how much disruption you had to go through to be here. The least I can do is make the transition a little ... comfortable."

I scowled across the horizon at the mountains, taken by surprise at how beautiful they were from here, a pale purple in the sweet May morning haze. I was stalemated, caught between the logic of her argument and my own gut resistance. "I ... I don't want to feel kept." An incoherent fragment of the dream that had roused me last night floated unpleasantly across my mind.

"You're not kept. Kept is when you're not free to go, you're beholden. You're always free to go. I know that. You don't need to walk miles barefoot to prove to me that you're your own woman. I wouldn't have dared asked you down here if I wasn't sure you were."

I walked to the back of the car, kicked a tire. Every moment with her had to be pressed. What else was she thinking, had she decided, that she wouldn't tell unless there was a confrontation? I was always forced out on a limb with her, and even then, she inched out only as far as she had to, to just barely brush me with her fingertips. "Well, I suppose I should say thank you, then."

She shrugged and walked around to the passenger side, running her hand along the roof. "I figured one less decision you had to make, the better. I sympathize. I have trouble with change myself."

This was how she did it, then, it struck me all at once. She focused on the details: what furniture should go in "my" room, which papers I should send my resumé to, what car I should drive, what routes I should learn. All those details and she could avoid the only things I seemed able to train my mind on at all: What did it mean that we shared a bed now but had never said "I love you?" What did she do when she was away days and weeks without me? Was I allowed to ask, allowed to feel jealous? How long was I here for, and if it wasn't forever — and how far off and fantastical such a notion seemed — why had I given up and left behind everything that had meant anything to me before?

"Will it do, then?"

I looked up. "What?"

"The car. Will it do?"

"It'll do for now," I said. "I'll start saving as soon as I get a job. I don't like to borrow. I like to own."

I pushed the cart up and down the supermarket aisles while Zena Beth examined the wares. She wore the wire-rimmed glasses again. She was leaving for Louisville tomorrow and wanted to make sure the cook — who would continue to take care of all the meals for just me — had everything she needed. So far, we had chicken cutlets and pork chops, tomatoes, fresh stringbeans, sugar, toilet paper and lightbulbs. Every time she lifted something off a shelf, I flinched. Each item, so ordinary and banal, seemed hardly worthy of her attention. As we went along, I felt more and more tortured with the need to think of something stimulating to talk about. I couldn't bear to be associated with toilet paper in the presence of Zena Beth Frazer.

She was studying the boxed rice choices while my stomach was in knots. Just then a blonde woman in black tights and a hot pink tank top whirled a full cart around the corner and nearly crashed into us.

"Oh migod," she said in a heavier accent than I'd heard since I'd been here. "Zena Beth, how *are* you?"

Zena Beth turned and worked her glasses off her nose. I could tell her smile was reluctant.

"Dotty. Fine, yourself?"

"Well, not so good since I haven't heard from you," she singsonged, inching her cart forward.

Zena Beth let her glance meet mine for a second

before she spoke. "Dotty, I'd like you to meet a friend of mine. This is Joyce Ecco. She's just moved down here from New York City."

"Well, well, a Yankee," Dotty said, putting out her hand. She was pretty and petite and younger than Zena Beth — but older than I. "Where are you living, child?" She let her eyes sweep over me from head to toe, taking me in like a cow up for auction.

"She's living with me, Dotty," Zena Beth said, her accent getting one fold richer.

"Oh, I see then. A real pleasure meeting you, I'm sure." She turned back to Zena Beth. "Well, *I'm* still livin' in the same place, darlin'," she said, before wheeling her cart squeakily away.

I stared after her, my heart slamming into my chest, as Zena Beth turned back to the rice. My mouth was so dry I couldn't speak.

"I'm sorry about that," Zena Beth said, reading the back of a brown box.

My temples were moist and my palms clammy. "You're *sorry?*" I said. "That's all you have to say?"

She looked up at me, twirling her glasses between two fingers the way she did, I knew now, when she was irritated. "What else did you have in mind?"

"Some explanation," I blurted.

"I think the conversation explained everything, don't you? Or were you looking to find out what our favorite positions had been?"

"Don't talk to me like I'm some rabid Italian mechanic from Staten Island. Answer the goddamn question." My jaw was clenched so tight my back teeth hurt. I saw her looking at me like I was crazy, someone to be escaped. I was vaguely terrified that I was talking to her this way.

"I don't believe I heard a question."

"Who was she. What was she to you. And how do I know it's over."

"She's one of the gym teachers at the local high school. We went to bed a few times over the last year or so. You know it's over because I said it's over." She tossed a box of rice into the cart and started down the aisle.

My back was sweating. I was at some kind of turning point and she had no idea. If I walked out of the store now, refusing to trail after her like some Chinese wife, I'd only have to wait by her car while she finished shopping. I had no other way to get back to the house. And who knew how long she could carry on in stony silence? Something told me a helluva lot longer than I could. And she was leaving tomorrow. It wasn't what I wanted. I wanted answers. I shoved the cart after her.

"Okay, since you don't seem to like my questions, why don't you answer your own?" I asked, my face hot with anger. "What *were* your favorite positions? That seems to be the medium you deal in, not emotions."

"I'm not going to respond to childish goading." She was gathering up a few six packs of cola.

"The woman obviously thought she meant something to you. *Did* she? Why can't I know these things about you?"

"I've told you about the last woman who meant something to me."

"Ad nauseam, thank you very much. But what about the others? They're the ones who scare me."

She was walking away. I grabbed her arm and turned her around. "Because I worry that I'm one of

them. One of the ones who think they mean
something to you."

Her face changed. I could see how she hated it,
hated to be called to the mat before she was ready.

"Am I down here for up-close inspection, some
bug under a microscope, while you decide if you can
fall in love with me?" My eyes blurred with tears.
"It's not fair, goddamn it, that I did it the other way
around."

"Don't do this," she said.

I shook my head, hiding my eyes from her. "Do
what? Which part?"

"Make demands. That's how we got this far.
Because you didn't."

It was astounding to me. No one had ever said
such things so baldly to me before. In every
relationship I'd been in up till then women had done
everything to disguise or rationalize their stinginess or
cruelty or duplicity. But here was Zena Beth, calmly
stating her right to all of hers.

The rest of what I was feeling I didn't say. That
what she called demands I called my needs. That
being loved didn't have to mean being caged and
being trapped. That loving someone didn't have to be
a contest of wills that you lost, or something that
would eventually hurt.

When we got to the checkout line, Dotty was
nowhere in sight.

"Pretty fancy resumé for someone applying for a
copy editor's job," Ross Tippey, the managing editor,
was saying. I had walked right by him when I first

came in because I would never have guessed that a
man in a T-shirt and jeans could be
second-in-command at the paper that was the largest
in the county.

"Well, that's the opening you have, isn't it? Your
job, for instance, is filled." I smiled.

He smiled back slowly and tossed the resumé on
his cluttered desk. "You want to tell me why you
chucked it all? Bright lights, big city and all of that?"

"You want the answer that gets the job, or you
want the truth?" I hadn't wasted any time figuring
out what took the edge off a Southerner's suspicions
of someone with a Yankee accent.

"I guess it depends on whether you want the job,
doesn't it?" He was smiling at his own joke,
smoothing his hand over his prematurely receding
hairline. I put him at about thirty, some eight years
older than I was.

"I came down here for a lifestyle change. And I
know I have to get acclimated to the surroundings
before I can be a decent reporter for you. So I'm
willing to take a copy editor's job till I get my
bearings. But then I hope you'll give me a shot at
reporting sooner than later."

"Was that the truth or the answer that gets the
job?"

"I guess it depends on whether you want to hire
me."

He had a deep, contagious laugh and I let myself
join in. "Well, I believe I do. Can you start
tomorrow?"

"Tomorrow's Saturday."

"That's right. We're a daily. Nothing fancy like a
weekly where you get the weekends off. And as low

woman on the totem pole, looks like you get to work prime time."

I smiled. It hardly mattered. Zena Beth's schedule didn't follow any pattern but her own whims, anyway. "Sure," I said, standing up. "I'll see you tomorrow, then, with my pencils sharpened."

"Well, you got your lifestyle change, at least."

— 11 —

When the doorbell rang shortly after I got home from my first day at the paper, I allowed myself the wild hope that it was Zena Beth, surprising me with the news that she hadn't gone to Louisville after all. No one else in town knew me. Nor was there anyone I could remotely imagine wanting to see.

"Luce!"

I hadn't seen her since that night at the 21 Club, and against the unfamiliar country night she looked like a long lost friend.

"Win any Pulitzers yet over at the T.C.?" T.C. was

the nickname for the paper. No locals ever called it
by its full name, the *Town Crier.*

"How did you know I was working there? Come
in, already," I said, shooing her off the porch.

"Well, I talked to your roommate today."

My face was to the door as I was shutting it, so
Luce couldn't see me flinch. Zena Beth hadn't called
me since she'd left yesterday.

"Roommate. I'll have to try that one," I said,
forcing myself not to sound as gloomy as I felt.

"Whoa," Luce said, brushing her hand over her
hair. "I thought we'd wait till we at least sat down
to dinner before we got to the heavy stuff."

"Oh, dinner. Good idea. There's stuff in the
fridge."

"Nonsense. I've got permission from the lady of
the house to take you out for a meal. It may not be
the big city, Joyce, but it's still Saturday night."

I scanned Luce's face for signs of a mercy visit,
but her light blue eyes looked genuinely welcoming
and pleased. And in her brown leather jacket and
cowboy boots, she made handsome company. I felt
my spirits lifting.

We hopped into her pickup truck, standard
driving equipment for men and women down here, it
seemed, and no clue to someone's sexual state of
mind, the way it was up north. Luce was amused by
my observation.

We pulled up to a place called the Swamp Side,
an innocuous-looking ranch that could have been
someone's home. It was amber-lit and smoky, loud
with the twang of country music and laughter. "It's
our local gay bistro," Luce shouted into my ear as a

grinning woman in a black leather vest and tight
jeans led us to a large booth. We slid onto the
wooden seats across from one another as the woman
handed us each a menu. "New in town, darlin'?" she
said to me, still grinning.

"You got that right, Marge," Luce answered for
me. "Living at the Frazer farm."

"No say?" Marge said, looking me over seriously.
"Well, you let us know what we can do to make
you feel welcome," she said, squeezing my shoulder
and walking off.

"Marge owns the place," Luce said. "Has, for
about twelve years."

"And no one bothers her?"

"Every once in a while you get some boys from
the high school who come in with their dates on a
dare, looking for a fight. Marge usually seats them —
which isn't what they bargained for — and they get
uptight enough in a few minutes that they leave on
their own."

I looked around, feeling cozy and happy, trying to
spot and recognize faces in the crowd. "Does Dotty
come here?"

Luce colored. "Dotty? How do you know Dotty?"

I told Luce the story, not quite ready to share all
the details of the fight, but hinting at enough.

"You know, the weeks are just as long down
here, if not longer, Joyce. You'll meet more than one
woman like Dotty. You can't be shocked every time
you trip over some woman Zena Beth's had a fling
with. Every lesbian in town knows where she lives."

"And evidently she knows where every one of
them lives, too."

Luce smiled maternally. "And she was so happy with all of them that she had to import you from the jungles of Manhattan."

I allowed myself to give in to a smile. "I just wanted to hear her say that."

"She's not going to, Joyce. I think you know that by now. But it's not a bad second to be happy with her actions. She did ask you here. And not Dotty or anyone else has lived in her house since Helena."

"It's tricky to read meaning into action. Not everyone acts the same way for the same reasons."

Luce sat back and drummed her fingers on the table. "I can't argue with that. But I *can* tell you that the catfish here is a knockout."

We ordered our meals and Luce got us both a glass of white wine. "Here's to my new neighbor," she toasted.

"Zena Beth didn't put you up to this, did she? I mean, you're not babysitting me when you could be out with some woman who's trying to get you horizontal?"

Luce pursed her lips. "Joyce, Zena Beth never puts me up to anything, least of all this. This is completely my pleasure."

And completely my idea, I saw her thinking. It apparently didn't cross Zena Beth's mind for a minute that I might be lonely and want company. But Luce was too polite — and too loyal — to say so.

"How is she, anyway? I haven't spoken to her since she left."

"Fine. It's the usual gig. She misses you. She was surprised how much." Luce was whispering.

"She didn't call me to say so," I said, my throat parched.

"Like I said."

While we ate, she asked me about the paper and how the first day went. I made her laugh describing the breaking news stories I had worked on about fertilizer prices and a blocked-up sewer. "The reporters seem a nice bunch, though. Most of them aren't much older than I. I guess they move after a year or two with a paper like T.C. Try to get on a big city paper."

"That's right — they go to Charlotte or Greensboro or Raleigh, if they can get it. Of course, plenty of them just leave the state altogether. Head up to Knoxville or Atlanta — or New York."

The gloom descended again. I was out of my element. I did not aspire to work my way through newspapers of the South. Zena Beth could work anywhere, and yet she had dug in her heels down here. Why had I made it so easy for her, jumping at her very first proposition?

"You know, Zena Beth's got this patch of earth in her blood," Luce said, reading my mind. "Do you know the story about Hercules wrestling Atlas? Where Atlas gains strength every time he's thrown to the ground? Well, Zena Beth's like that. Her identity is all tied up with her farm, this town, the South. You wouldn't like her for long out of her element, anyway. Just the travel makes her edgy."

"What's going to happen with us, Luce?" I asked, rubbing my temples. "I haven't even got a map."

"Just ride it out. You're down here now. Anything could happen. Anything."

That was what I was afraid of.

* * * * *

When Luce left, the silence of the large, empty house pressed in all around me. I'd slept alone the night before but I was so anxious about my first day at the paper that I hadn't had time to notice anything else. Tonight I thought I wouldn't be able to bear it. I crawled under the covers, clutching Zena Beth's pillow, faint with her fragrance, and dialed Nikki.

"Thank God you're home," I said, when she answered on the first ring.

"Joyce? Hey, this is great. But what the hell are we both doing home on a Saturday night?"

I quickly brought her up to date and then put the question to her.

"Well, here's the deal. Caryn goes on her date with fiancé Bob, then she tells him she can't stay over — some big family event the next morning. Then she drives herself over here to spend the night. I expect her in about two hours."

"Nikki, I can't believe you're doing this to yourself."

"Joyce, please. Don't lecture. You know I'm kicking myself. But I haven't met a woman I've felt this way about in ... too long. I'm going to be patient with her."

I sighed loudly, scanning the empty room and deciding I didn't have any right to lecture anyone about playing it safe. "Well, Jesus Christ. I hope you're at least taking precautions. This is a woman we *know* is sleeping with a man. And God knows who else *he's* sleeping with."

"Yeah, yeah."

"What does she say about all this?" I asked.

"She's mostly focused on the idea that she's cheating on him — and he's pressing her to set a wedding date. She's not thinking too much about the fact that she's cheating with a woman, not a man."

"How convenient."

"Meaning?" Nikki asked, sounding defensive.

"Meaning that's a nice smokescreen. Of course it makes all the difference in the world that she's cheating with a woman."

"Well, to you and me it does."

"But if this is a woman who you say is on the brink of coming out, it ought to make some difference to her, too. Come on, Nikki, you're going too easy on her."

"She's freaked out, Joyce. She says the sex with me is a hundred times better than with him."

Nikki laughed but I could hear it was getting to her. I said, "*You* should be out on another date while you're waiting for her to finish up with fiancé Bob."

"Sometimes I do. I went out last weekend. In fact, I saw Elaine again."

It still happened. Every time I heard her name it was like someone dropped hot coals on my head. "She was out with the same woman again?"

"Yeah. They looked pretty cozy."

"Shit. Don't tell me any more. Don't tell me any details," I said.

"I didn't tell you any last time. You just assumed. I told you that you didn't want to know the truth. You're just as bad as I am, Joyce."

"No wonder we can't help each other."

"No, you're wrong about that. I feel better already. Jesus, I miss you. It's a bitch."

I strained to hold back tears. I was in exile, self-imposed. My life was going on without me. "I

have to see this through, Nikki. Sometimes I feel like
... like I'm getting to her, like she needs me but she
can't admit it. Her letters are the only thing ... her
letters and the way she makes love to me. If it
weren't for that ..." I trailed off, too stirred by the
memory of her hands and lips on me to go on.

"Hey, Joyce — you okay?"

"Yeah. Yeah, I'm fine. Look, I should get going.
This working weekends stuff is wearing me down."

But when we hung up, I couldn't sleep at all.

The mail came early, while the house was
humming with various workers — the stable boy, the
cook, the cleaning woman, the gardener. Evidently
they had all been told I would be there, because
they greeted me by name and treated me
deferentially, as if I were paying their salaries as
much as Zena Beth was. I felt like a complete fraud.

The cleaning woman had scooped up the mail to
leave in Zena Beth's office, except for one pale blue
envelope addressed to me that she left on the
kitchen table, next to a glass of orange juice and a
selection of cereals. My heart raced as I tore open
the envelope.

Dear Joyce:

*I'm writing this on the plane to Louisville.
I'm sorry I can't be there for your first day
at the new job, but I know you'll be great.
You'll be running the place within the month.
I wonder if they know what they've gotten
into.*

I held myself back from asking you to come with me on this trip. I didn't because I knew you wouldn't be able to come on all of them, and I didn't want to get spoiled. I would never dream of asking anyone to give up her work — if you're like me, you'd die without it — but if you end up hating this job, I just want you to know that you don't have to keep it.

What I hate is being on the road alone. I distract myself by getting at least a whiff of the city or town I'm in, but it isn't nearly as much fun as sharing it with someone. Most of the time, I'm able to forget about it, but having you in the house, in bed next to me, reminded me all over again.

I think a lot of people assume that success fills up your life. But I've been at this long enough to tell you that while it takes up your time, it doesn't fill up your life. Of course, it's nicer to be rich and lonely than poor and lonely — I'll be the first to attest to that — but it's lonely nonetheless. People come to you bubbling with curiosity — not the least of which is sexual — and you feel you can't trust a soul. You're never anonymous, never without your reputation. In the end, the work has to be your best friend.

Love,
Zena Beth

I reread the letter a few more times, till I felt sure I knew its rhythms and secrets, before I folded it back up and returned it to its envelope. How she doled herself out in tiny portions, always behind a screen of words — mannered, practiced, and controlled, nothing as spontaneous or messy as face-to-face. But, I told myself, it was better than nothing.

Sliding into my battered swivel chair on day two was a lot more comfortable than it had been on day one. Already I felt a kind of vague belonging, already I had come to think of the T.C. as "our" paper, rather than theirs. I knew people's names when I said good morning, instead of having to introduce myself. Maybe I could pull this off.

Ross had a pile of stories waiting in my in-box to be copy-edited. I picked them up casually, expecting perhaps a cat rescue or the birth of triplets. So the story on top took me totally by surprise.

"An unprecedented gay rights bill up for city council vote next month appears in danger of defeat already, due to the loud and spirited attack launched by Councilmember Louise Fleck," the story began. It went on to explain how the bill would make workplace discrimination illegal — and would require extending insurance benefits to the partners of gay and lesbian employees. Evidently it was the insurance issue that had sent feathers flying. The top brass of local businesses complained that such a requirement would cost them extra money. Worse, they complained, gay couples were known not to stay together long, and it wasn't fair that the companies had to "subsidize a string of some fag's boyfriends," one unidentified manager was quoted as saying.

Councilwoman Fleck, the story went on, (I corrected it to councilmember for consistency with the paper's style), had come out on the side of the businesses, charging further that the bill "discriminated against heterosexual couples who chose to live together, and was an affront to the morals of county residents. 'No one's stopping these couples from living together, but this bill asks us to underwrite a lifestyle that a majority objects to,' " she was quoted as saying yesterday.

I carried the story, my hand shaking slightly, into Ross's office. He was typing furiously on his computer terminal, his back to me.

"Ross," I said, knocking. "Can I ask you a question?"

He whirled around, looking as though I had caught him in some private, deeply hedonistic act. "Yeah. Morning, Joyce."

"Is uh —" I glanced at the byline on the story — "Sue Havermill in today?"

"Nope. Sue won't be in till Tuesday again, I believe. Why?"

"Oh, I just wanted to tell her that I liked her story. And —"

"Yeah?" He leaned back, settling in for a chat. "Have a seat." He gestured at the chair on the other side of his desk.

"I was curious about who sponsored the bill. The story doesn't say."

"Lemme see." He scanned it. "Yeah, you're right.

It should. We covered it when it first came up, a few weeks back. Check the morgue. I'm pretty sure it was Richards. Rich Richards. Liberal member of the council. Black guy. Good catch, Joyce. That all?"

My scalp tingled; so the bill had two major strikes against it already, I suspected. Its content, and a black sponsor.

"Well, yes, technically." I stood up. "But you're busy. I'll come back."

"News can't wait on a daily, Joyce. What's on your mind?" He put his hands behind his head and smiled broadly.

I sat back down. "Well, I just wondered if you had other coverage planned. Something makes me feel there's a bigger story here than meets the eye. What I mean is, what about a profile of Richards and another of — what's her name — Fleck? I think it'd be fascinating to know something about their backgrounds and how they came to be on such opposite sides of an issue like this. And this is really on the cutting edge of employment law, Ross. I mean, New York's been trying to pass a bill like this for years. For a Sunday edition, I mean — when we'd have more space."

"Hmmmmm," he said, twisting his gold stretch watchband. "People around here pretty well know who Richards and Fleck are —"

"Well, maybe they think they do, Ross. People get reduced to a few bare facts when all you get to hear about them is an attribution line after an angry quote. Maybe we don't really know them."

He rubbed his cheek; I could hear from across the desk that he needed a shave. "But why this bill, Joyce? Plenty of bills come and go that have a whole lot more to do with most people's lives than this one."

"Because this one gets people hot under the collar. This is the one people are going to be arguing about in bars."

"And because you live at the Frazer farm?"

I clutched my stomach; I literally felt I'd been kicked in the gut. How had I left myself so wide open? How had I let myself believe I was among fellow journalists, even friends? It was another rotten-to-the-core, closed-minded, small-town paper.

"How do you know that?" I demanded when I got my breath back.

"You filled out the application form, remember? I know the address of the Frazer farm."

"Wait a minute. You recognized the address even before you called me in for an interview?"

"That's right. And I hired you anyway, as I recall. Just because I talk funny to you doesn't make me a redneck bigot, Joyce. And I'm still a working journalist." He gestured to the computer screen behind him. "I'm trained to notice details, not to let a nuance go by. I don't care who you sleep with. But I care about this paper looking like its got an agenda. How long do you think it'll take for word to get around that I've got Zena Beth Frazer's new girlfriend working for my paper if we start giving front-page coverage to this little bill and raking Louise Fleck over the coals? Don't you remember your classes in the *appearance* of conflict of interest?"

"Yes, I do. I also remember them in separation of church and state. What you're trying not to say is that you've graduated to the level where you have to worry about losing advertisers. And the advertisers are

all the businesses who want this bill to be DOA
when the vote comes up."

"What I'm saying is give me some hard-news
reason to make a bigger deal out of this story, Joyce.
But until then, I'm not going on fishing expeditions
in print. And if you turn something up, I still can't
let you cover it, anyway." He fiddled with his
watchband again. "Get me something good, though,
and I'll feed it to Sue. And I'll consider it as you
paying your dues."

"Fair enough," I said, standing up. "I don't think
you'll be disappointed."

It wasn't the first dream I'd had about Elaine
since I'd come to Mountville, but this one didn't
dissolve the way the others had once I emerged
more fully into wakefulness.

We were in Elaine's kitchen in Brooklyn,
preparing a feast, but there were no guests besides
us. The table was set elaborately with vibrant,
colorful china and gleaming silverware. The two of us
were slightly damp with the effort of chopping and
peeling, stirring and seasoning. We were laughing and
feeding each other morsels, pausing to kiss or do a
single twirl to the music on in the background, and
suddenly I started to cry. "It'll never be ready," I said
over and over. Elaine looked on, wooden spoon in
hand, her brow creased with fear and confusion.
That's all I remembered.

It was early; Elaine would not have left for work

yet. Still under the covers, I reached for the phone, nearly feeling her lips on mine, her hand in my hand, burning to tell her ... to tell her anything, to say that it was as if no time or torment had passed between us, that nothing I ever did or nowhere I ever went would change a thing between us.

"Hello?" she asked expectantly.

I smiled hard, joy welling up in me like a pressure. It seemed like a miracle, to have this small, secret pleasure of her voice in my ear, however fleeting.

"Hello?" she asked again. "Who is it?" Impatience and curiosity were fighting each other in her voice, I could hear it, and I longed to break my silence, to answer her, to say all the things we used to say. Then grief, like a spasm, stopped me, and I lowered the receiver back into place with excruciating care.

— 12 —

I had been pacing in front of the window for a half hour before Zena Beth's white Jaguar turned into the driveway, throwing up dust and gravel. She was out of the car before I made my way down to her, and the sight of her serious, elegant profile melted all my resistance. How had I lasted these few days without her, I wondered.

"Hi, gorgeous," I said, throwing my arms around her from behind — and immediately feeling her stiffen.

"Let's save the physical displays for inside," she

said, turning around to smile tightly. "The neighbors like me within certain bounds. No fucking on the front lawn, for instance."

The same rage I had felt in the supermarket bubbled to the surface immediately. "If you think that was fucking, darlin'," I said, aping her accent, "you've been away too long."

She was pulling her garment bag out of the trunk but dropped it to the ground in a fit of laughter. "Well, I see the sweet country air has mellowed you in my absence," she said, grinning at me as if I were a precocious child.

I studied her in her hunter-green riding pants and black-and-red checkered blouse. Against the mountains in the horizon and the newly lush trees, she looked completely in her element. I longed for her, worshipped her, even, and yet she could pierce me the way no other woman ever had. I had felt returned to my own skin the last few days, and now I was instantly back under her spell. It was both enraging and intoxicating. Just watching her, my whole body was warming and softening, welcoming her, craving her.

I helped her carry her bags up the stairs, even though she was strong enough to carry all of them, and me included. As usual, I felt a need to make myself useful in some way to her. I sat on her bed as she unpacked and told me random details about the flight, the theater group, the play, the meals they had fed her, the conversations she had had.

"I brought you a little something," she said, holding out a box.

Inside was a black Montblanc pen. I could barely meet her eyes. "It's too much, as usual," I said. "But

it's beautiful. Thank you." I got up and kissed her
lightly, slowly, on both eyelids, on both cheeks, then
on the lips.
"I need a shower," she said.
I pulled away, feeling rebuked.
"No, come with me." She took my hand and led
me to the bathroom.
I watched her as she adjusted the water and
turned the shower on full blast. She was out of her
clothes just as the mirrors started to steam up.
"Aren't you coming?" she asked, unzipping my jeans
and impatiently working the buttons of my shirt.
We stepped over the pile of clothes and embraced
under the hard rush of the hot shower. She threw
the curtain closed around us, enclosing us in a
roaring, steamy privacy. As the shower poured
furiously over our faces, we kissed like madwomen,
gulping down air and water, pushing away strands of
plastered hair, dark and silken, nearly losing our
balance on the slippery ceramic floor as we angled to
press our hips and thighs together.
Zena Beth reached for the soap and slowly
worked it over my back and buttocks, not stopping
her kisses. She cupped the bar and moved it carefully
over my neck and nipples, then glided it between my
legs. I struggled to keep my knees locked, uncertain I
could remain standing. I was stunned and dizzy with
desire, the pound of the shower, and the swift and
sure movement of her hands and lips, which seemed
to be everywhere at once.
She moved alongside me, biting my neck, and
crowded both hands between my legs as the shower
hit me full in the face. "God, you're so open for
me," she breathed, pressing her fingers deep inside

me till I felt such exquisite pressure I thought I
would explode. Her other hand was closing in with
narrower and narrower circles. Even the muscles in
my calves had gone weak and tingly. "You can
stand," she promised throatily, feeling me buck
against her as my knees gave way. Her finger flicked
the swollen place just once before release ripped
through me, making me call out, my voice bouncing
off the tiled shower walls. She pressed me hard
against her, holding me up, cradling the back of my
head with her hand, and I found myself crying, my
face hot and tight with tears against her shoulder.

"I love you," I choked out, feeling remorse and
relief all at once. "I love you. I can't help it. It's just
true."

She swayed us both slowly, as the shower
continued to wash loudly over us. "Shhhh, shhhh,"
she said, running her hand lightly over my forehead
and hair, squeaky with water.

We stood that way for several minutes till I
collected myself. I felt bruised from the inside out
and pulled her cautiously down to the floor, letting
her rest her back against the curved far end of the
tub. I pushed her bent legs apart roughly while the
water spilled off my back onto her thighs. I took her
in my mouth, licking languidly, sucking lightly, and
then moved aside so the rush of the shower rained
down hard on her. Her eyes were closed and she
was thrashing her head back and forth, alternately
cursing and praising me, pleading or cajoling. "Get
inside me," she commanded finally, and I did, taking
her in my mouth again, too, feeling her thrust up at
me, matching my rhythm, until she called out, her

whole body tensed as if against a blow, before slowing to a tremble.

I curled on the floor between her legs, my head on her stomach, my knees squeezed against the side of the tub. The water continued to crash down on us, blocking out all other sound, even thought. "Be patient with me," she said over the din, her hands resting on my back. "I'm afraid of the other words . . . but God, you move me." We lay there, listening to the roar of the shower till we could stand it no more.

We were shy with each other the rest of the night. A low murmur of happiness, a peaceful, bone-deep calm, overtook me. I sensed that Zena Beth felt it, too. She made us tea after dinner and suggested we sit in bed together and just cuddle and watch TV.

"What do you know about Louise Fleck on the city council?" I asked after something on the news jogged my memory.

"Louise? That she's a dyke."

"*What?* That's impossible!" I'd been resting against Zena Beth's breast, but now I sat up. "She's on a campaign to defeat the gay rights bill."

"Why impossible? There's no dyke more dangerous than a closeted dyke," Zena Beth said. "Not to sound full of myself, but the only reason she won't try to sleep with me is because she knows I won't tolerate that shit. She only hits on women so awed by her power and position they wouldn't tell

on penalty of death. Or women who have just as
much reason to want to keep it a secret. I don't fall
into either category, you see."

I was reeling with this new information, holding
myself back from rushing to the phone to call Ross.
"How do you know all this?"

"Darlin', *everyone* knows. She doesn't make a
secret of it. She doesn't have to. The papers won't
dare print an allegation that someone is gay, not even
if they had the proof in eight-by-ten glossies. It's still
one of the worst things you can be called and it
practically guarantees a lawsuit. You can call a
politician a liar and a cheat and a racist, and they'll
calmly issue a statement saying why it's not true. But
call someone a fag or a dyke, and they'll sue your ass
from here to the Mason-Dixon line."

"So what do you mean? All the local media
knows, too?"

"Well, I can't say that. But everyone in the gay
community knows. She even goes to the Swamp Side
and I'm not saying people buy her beers, but no one
hassles her, either. Because enough people in town
don't want it broadcast that *they're* in the Swamp
Side, either. So she's protected on both ends."

I was having a hard time taking this all in. "But
what about now? Even when she's openly attacking
the gay community? I mean, we're quoting her saying
things like it offends God and nature."

"I'm sure it offends her, too. She'd much rather
be straight, and if she could take a pill for it, she
probably would. She's safely married and widowed,
and some of the women she takes to bed are wives
of her political cronies. So no one's rushing to get on
Oprah, if you follow me."

"I can't believe this. And you're just going to stand by and take it while she single-handedly defeats this bill?"

"Joyce, what can *I* do that I'm not already doing just by being completely visible and vocal about my own life? But none of the papers are rushing to interview me about Louise Fleck. They wouldn't believe what I had to say about her if I had her pubic hair stuck between my teeth. I am simply not an impartial — read believable — source, don't you see?"

I was beginning to, and it was depressing the hell out of me.

"Actually, I find your outrage kind of funny, Joyce, considering that you're not out to your parents or anyone you've ever worked with."

"That's not a fair comparison," I protested, feeling my cheeks color. "I never laughed at gay jokes. I didn't try to fool people. And I sure as hell didn't go out of my way to attack other gay people just to make sure no one suspected me."

"Safe is safe, Joyce. Some people in some settings have to go further to throw off suspicion."

It was all I could do to hold her stare; being in the high beam of Zena Beth's ridicule, even at its mildest, was withering. "So you're saying that those of us who are silent are just as guilty."

"I can't take credit for the sentiment 'If you're not with me, you're against me.' Someone beat me to it by about a thousand years."

I felt as if this was some kind of test. All those early, innocent queries about whether or not I minded being seen with her on the street had not been so idle, perhaps. Maybe what she ultimately

wanted was someone to loudly claim her, to keep
pace with her politics. Maybe she needed to feel that
the woman beside her in bed was willing to take on
the whole world just to be with her.

"Everyone has a different breaking point," I said.
"Everyone gets shoved till she says stop. But
sometimes you don't know your limit till you're
down on your ass."

"Now there's a proverb I can warm up to," she
said, smiling and reaching out for me.

I folded gratefully into her embrace, vowing to do
something, somehow, that would win even just a
little bit of her respect.

Sue Havermill and I sat across a table at the local
diner where most of the T.C. staff went for lunch if
they didn't brown bag it.

"Yeah, Ross drives a hard bargain when it comes
to things like this," Sue was saying, biting into her
burger. She was a big woman with an unruly halo of
black hair, newly and happily married, and unafraid
to call herself a feminist and a liberal. All this she
offered in the three minutes it took us to get from
the office to the diner. "He doesn't go for kamikaze
tactics. *The New York Post* wouldn't exactly be
clamoring to sign him on."

"I understand that, but sometimes the news just
doesn't come to you. You have to go and get it."

"Bottom line is, Ross isn't going to do a profile
on Fleck if all we do is hint around that she's a
flaming hypocrite. Her resumé is too good. Her
connections are too good."

"What are we supposed to do? Carry a concealed camera into the Swamp Side?"

Sue's eyes widened. "That's it —"

"Sue, I was kidding."

"No, no. Too problematic. Entrapment. Besides, it doesn't prove a thing. What we need is a flesh-and-blood source. Can you find out who some of Fleck's lady loves — past or present — are?"

"I'm pretty sure I could. Yeah."

"Think they'd talk?"

"On the record?"

"You don't really think Ross's going to publish an accusation as explosive as this from a source who won't be named."

"Shit," I said, shaking my head. "What's in it for the woman? Why in hell would anyone stick her neck out like that? Besides, from what I hear, most of the women she chooses are as closeted as she is."

Sue leaned across the table. "Rule number one. Someone will always talk. You just gotta figure out what motivates them. And then make them think they're about to be a goddamn hero."

"Sounds like a con game to me."

"Hey, it's for the greater good, right? You can't be squeamish in this business. Of course, we can play it safe, play by Ross's rules. And then watch the bill go down the tubes — and Louise Fleck sail into another term, hypocrisy and the American way intact."

"You drive a hard bargain, too."

"Now you sound like my husband," Sue said.

* * * * *

"What're you doing?" I asked, hovering in the doorway of Zena Beth's study, where she sat at her desk.

She looked over the top of her glasses. "Working on my play."

I stepped into the room. "Play? You never told me you had started a new play."

"Bad luck to talk about it. Breaks the tension."

"So why'd you tell me now?" She had put her arms out and I walked into them.

"You asked."

"You are a mystery," I said, running my hand through her hair, watching the light catch the scatter of gray. "I guess you don't want to say what it's about."

"I'm not really sure I know yet."

I was willing to wager that I did. Helena was at the top of my list. I could see the ghosts in Zena Beth's eyes.

"I guess it's about the way we measure our connections to each other," she said, uneasy; I could tell it from the guarded way she pushed her papers and pen around. "You know, it doesn't shock me that so many people split up, divorce. It shocks me that anyone ever stays together."

My scalp tingled with fear and dread.

"What I mean is," she continued, "the only really irrevocable tie is parent to child. Especially mother to child. You came from my body. Where can you run to hide from that? Nowhere, not the ends of the earth. But romantic love? With or without the legal documents — how ridiculous, really, to think that might make a difference. What are you when it's over? A former. A negative. A nothing."

That's what irked her the most, I knew. The lack
of any legitimate claim to Helena. And now she
wasn't even the ex. She was one of the exes. "Have
you spoken to Helena recently?" I asked, moving out
of the circle of her arms.

"Actually," she said, turning her back to her desk,
"I saw her in Louisville."

"Oh?" I said mildly, though I felt myself go red to
the roots of my hair. "I didn't know they had much
skiing there this time of year."

"She donated some money to open an athletics
center for girls and they invited her to cut the
ribbon."

"So you had dinner together?"

"Yes, dinner." She shuffled some pages on her
desk.

"So how is she? She and Lila?"

"Lila wasn't with her, but she says they're
deliriously happy."

"You never believe her, though, do you?"

She met my eyes, taking measure. "It's not
narcissism. I just know her. And she isn't a very
good judge of people."

I feigned sleepiness and left the room. This was
no longer a safe topic for the two of us to discuss, I
saw. I couldn't trust myself. Worse, I saw that I
couldn't trust her.

— 13 —

No way, not till hell freezes over," the woman across the table from Luce and me was saying.

Luce had agreed to come with me to the Swamp Side to look for and talk to any of Louise Fleck's formers about the clash between her public opinion and her private life. As an outsider, especially one connected to the newspaper, I wouldn't have gotten far without her, we'd both agreed. I clamped my hands together tightly on the table, and let Luce do the talking.

"You've read the things she's been saying in the paper, Martha, haven't you?"

"Yeah, I have. And we used to fight about that stuff when we were together, too. I didn't get anywhere with her then. And I don't expect to now." She pushed her red bangs across her forehead.

"She could make such a big difference if she spoke out for the bill, Martha," Luce said patiently.

"She could also watch her career go down the sewer. Are we gonna be the ones to turn in our own kind?"

I couldn't stay quiet any longer. "But she turned on you — on all of us — first, don't you think?"

"I don't think she did a damn thing to you, young lady. How long are you living down here, anyway? Twenty minutes?"

Luce shot me an exasperated look before reaching across the table to pat Martha's hand. "Now, now. I know she was good to you, Martha —"

"You're damn right she was." Her round cheeks had colored. "I was out of work for a few months and she made sure I didn't end up living on the street. And she always treated me right every other way. I didn't expect her to go passing bills just so we could sleep together."

I kicked Luce under the table. This was going nowhere fast. And I was in danger of losing my temper.

"Well, I see your point of view, Martha. But you let me know if you change your mind and come around to seeing mine, okay?"

"Sure. But I wouldn't quit drinking while I was waiting, Luce," Martha said, standing up and playfully punching Luce's shoulder. "And no offense to you, either,'' she said to me. "I remember what it was like to be young. Think you can change the world and everything. You'll get over that, too."

I smiled tightly and managed to keep my mouth shut.

Back at the house, Zena Beth fixed us all a drink. She and Luce hadn't seen each other in weeks, and they were visibly happy to be in each other's company. Luce was one of the few women I could watch Zena Beth be near and not feel raw with jealousy.

"So, have the two of you toppled the evil empire yet?" Zena Beth asked, putting her feet up on the leather ottoman. She massaged the bridge of her nose, which I knew meant she had been in her office, writing.

"Oh yeah, we're within reach," Luce said, squeezing my knee and laughing. "Marge thought Martha Sikes was going to be our best bet — and if she was our best, I think we ought to go congratulate Louise Fleck right now. Cheers!" Luce raised her glass in a mock toast.

"Oh ye of little faith," Zena Beth said. "You haven't seen Joyce when she gets determined. She gets like one of the horses. 'Move me, I dare you,' she says."

Zena Beth was smiling affectionately at me; I knew by now that a comparison to Atlantis or Ziegfeld was a heartfelt compliment. I wrestled back the urge to squeeze next to her on the chair and bury my face in her neck and hair. The last thing I wanted was to make Luce feel unwelcomed and besides, I knew it would strike Zena Beth as odd or inappropriate. I had begun to notice that she rarely touched me, except as a prelude to sex.

"Of course, you could always sleep with her, Luce, as long as you kept a recording device in your bra," Zena Beth said.

"That's out — you know I never wear a bra," Luce teased back.

"I feel bad about it, though," I said. "These are women who are keeping quiet because they have to. They need to keep their jobs. They don't want rocks through their windows at night."

"Sometimes a rock through the window at night is the breath of fresh air that someone closeted needs," Zena Beth said. "As long as we run from being named, we tell them they can use the facts of our lives against us, again and again."

"Yeah but how come it's always just the select few who have to pick glass out of their underwear?" Luce asked.

"Well, I'd rather be one of the ones who did the work for everyone than sit back and have no one benefit. But then, I guess that's obvious. But I have to tell you, it's great to have all the help I can get." She took in me and Luce with a contented glance.

"Well, I'm off," Luce said, getting up and stretching. "All this work for the revolution is wearing me out." She winked and Zena Beth blew her a kiss.

"I'll walk you out," I said. I enjoyed playing hostess in the big house.

From the porch, we could see hot pink clouds blazing like liquid fire along the tops of the Smokies as the sun set. "It was fun working the bar with you," Luce said, smiling.

"Likewise." Luce was becoming my friend, not just Zena Beth's, and I liked it.

"Zena Beth looks well. I think you agree with her."

"Thanks, I feel pretty lucky."

"No," Luce said, "I think she's the one who's lucky." And then she bounded down the wooden steps and out to the road.

Ross pulled up a chair, backwards, in front of my desk and sat down, resting his forearms on the back of it. "I hear you're kicking up some dust, Joyce," he said.

I looked up warily from my copy editing. "What do you mean?"

"Oh, I just got a call from Councilmember Fleck's office," he said. "They were just wondering how we all were."

"I take it that's unusual."

"I knew you were a quick study." Ross was looking at me steadily, amusement and anxiety fighting for dominance on his thin face.

"This could be big, Ross. It's not just Mountville. This goes on all over the country. It could be a precedent-setting kind of story."

"I'm not sure we need to set precedent, Joyce. We just need to report the news as it's happening."

"This *is* the news as it's happening, Ross. This is reporting on how everyone looks the other way. How can a newspaper be in collusion with that?"

He raised an eyebrow. "Let me put it this way, Joyce. I don't want to get another phone call from Fleck's office, unless she's returning one of mine." He got up. "Otherwise, keep up the good work."

"It's unbelievable, it's like she's got moles," I said to Zena Beth about my conversation with Ross. "Because clearly someone went back and told Fleck that we were asking around." I was sitting on the edge of the bed and watching her pack. This time it would be a longer trip, to Seattle, to talk with theater producers there who wanted to do a local production of *Dykes and Other Strangers.*

"It was probably Martha. Women, in particular, are guilty of a kind of industrial-strength loyalty after they've slept with someone," Zena Beth said, surveying the clothes she'd laid out versus the size of her suitcase. "I've come to think it's chemical."

An oddly timed revelation, I thought, considering that we had just made love and she had pulled away, dispassionately, to pack. It was never far from surfacing, her open disdain for affection.

"What really went wrong between you and Helena?" I blurted.

She straightened up from the suitcase and looked at me. "I really don't want to talk about it. Besides, there's nothing coherent to say. Technically, she left me for Christine. But another woman is never the reason. Not really."

"What is, then?"

"Two people, two adults, have different fantasies of what it's going to be like to be in love, and when

you suddenly slam up against reality at some point in
an affair, you decide that the other person betrayed
you. When all along, you were only kidding yourself."
    Her words seemed to cast a pall over the room; I
was nearly afraid to move. Which of them, I
wondered — Helena or Zena Beth — had been kidding
herself? And what about me? Was it the fantasy of
Zena Beth Frazer that I still nursed, preferring it to
the more prickly, somehow less satisfying reality?
    She tucked the last of her clothes in the bag and
sat down on the bed next to me. "Will you be all
right?"
    "Of course," I said. How could I tell her that
sometimes I felt just as alone when she was right
beside me?
    "Good. You're your own woman, Joyce. That's an
asset. I think I'm going to turn in early. My flight's at
seven."
    She was at her most unsentimental at leave-taking;
maybe it was her way of coping with separation. Or
maybe it was just selfishness, putting herself at the
center of her universe, not stopping to weigh anyone
else's needs against her own. But the worst was, I
would never know which it was. I couldn't bring
myself to ask her, and I was even less capable of
judging.
    "I think I'll go down the hall and read for a
while," I said, knowing that the light bothered her
after she decided it was time to sleep. "Wake me
when you leave in the morning, okay?"
    "That seems silly," she said as she slipped out of
her jeans. "It'll be so early and tomorrow's your day
to sleep late."
    The more she pulled away, the harder I had to

fight not to cling. "You're right," I said. "It is silly."
And I closed the door behind me.

There are no great thunderclaps of revelation, no
mornings when you wake up and find all your
answers on your lap like breakfast brought to you in
bed. Most of the time, we discover that our decisions
have been made several weeks or even years before
we have the courage to face them; it only remains,
then, to find a way to rationalize them.

Zena Beth didn't say goodbye before she left, and
when I did wake up, close to nine, I found myself
thinking of Elaine. I had come a long way from home
to realize that I loved her . . . and to realize that that
wasn't enough. I still wanted to be Zena Beth
Frazer's lover enough to bear being miserable at it,
and even seeing the facts clearly was not enough to
persuade me to change course. Zena Beth was
wrong. I was not my own woman.

— 14 —

I hear you're looking for someone to talk," the woman's voice said when I picked up the phone. I hardly ever got a call at work, so for a second I wasn't even sure the call was meant for me.

"That's right," I said slowly. "Who is this?"

"I believe we've met. This is Dotty Oakes."

I was drawing a blank at first. "Dotty? From the supermarket?"

"That's right, child."

"How did you hear?"

"How does anyone? Isn't the important thing that I want to talk?"

"You understand the terms? That it's on the record?"

"I do."

"Why would you want to do it, Dotty? Especially being a teacher?"

"Because I'm blowing this two-bit town. And in my family, we like to go out with a bang. We like to be remembered."

"You'll have to tell me the story first."

"There ain't a whole lot to tell. It was a one-night stand. We met at the Swamp Side. We both had too much to drink. We never talked again after that morning. It wasn't what you call pretty. It isn't the nice sweet love story you mighta had in mind."

I did my best to ignore her digs. And I couldn't think of anything else to ask her. I knew the most important facts now: she would say she slept with Louise Fleck, and she would say it on the record. "Look, I'll have to work out the details here, Dotty. Can I have a phone number to call you back?"

She gave me a number. "That's the number at school, honey. I don't give out my home number to just anyone." And then she hung up.

Luce met me outside the T.C. building right after I called her. I relayed the details of Dotty's call as we walked to my car.

"It feels like a setup," Luce said as soon as she closed the passenger door.

"What do you mean?"

"I can't tell you exactly how," she said, looking more agitated than I'd ever seen her. "I'm not as evil as some of these people. But small town politics are as mean as in a big city, don't kid yourself. It could be something crazy, like —"

"Like what?" I demanded. I was too distracted to drive so we just sat by the curb.

"I don't know — like Fleck decided you weren't going to back off so she bought herself a decoy in the form of Dotty Oakes, who has a grudge against Zena Beth. So she can tell her story in print — and then later recant it so you and the paper look bad. Or so Fleck herself can come forward with evidence to show it's horseshit. Or so Dotty can say yes and then stall for weeks, taking you off the trail of other live ones. I don't know — use your imagination. All I know is, nothing falls into your lap this easy."

Luce was looking out the window like a fugitive. I could see it was killing her to have to disappoint me and not be celebratory. "And what if you're just being paranoid? What if this *is* the big story — and Fleck gets the last laugh because we walk away from it?"

"It's not the kind of story you want to be wrong about, Joyce. And Dotty just isn't the most upright citizen in town. At least, that's what everyone thinks."

I scowled out at the street and pounded the steering wheel. "Damn. Goddamn. What am I going to do?"

"It depends on whether you're planning on living here a while. And I sure hope you are." She squeezed my shoulder.

"It's hard for a person who likes the facts to have
to rely on instinct."

"Instinct's more reliable," Luce said, smiling.
"Everyone comes to see that sooner or later."

After dinner I sat in bed paging through a local
paper that listed nothing but used cars for sale. I had
tried to sit in the study or living room but those
rooms remained alien; nothing of Zena Beth's spirit
seemed present there.

The prices of cars that looked even remotely
reliable were still wildly out of my reach but I kept
scanning anyway. Every day that I drove the Saab I
felt more and more uncomfortable. There was enough
imbalance in our relationship already without
underscoring it daily with the car.

Halfway through the paper, I realized I wasn't
concentrating. I was thinking about Dotty instead.
Luce suggested I just not call back, but that didn't
feel right to me. What if Dotty *was* telling the truth?
She deserved some explanation. Like Luce said,
especially if I planned to live here a while.

She had given me only the school number, I
remembered, but suddenly I couldn't bear to wait
another minute before I put the whole business
behind me. I had seen Zena Beth use her address
book more than once and knew she kept it in the
night table on her side of the bed. I hesitated only a
moment before I took it out and started flipping the
pages to "O" in search of Dotty's home number. A
letter came shooting forward out of the book.

I tried to put it right back without even glancing,

but face-to-face with my neediness and curiosity, I caved in. I folded it open and saw an unfamiliar handwriting — childlike, highly rounded, easy to read. It was dated a few days before Zena Beth had left for Seattle.

Dear Zena Beth,

    I knew I wouldn't have a chance to talk to you for some time, and I didn't want to let this sit and simmer. What happened can't happen again. There really is something to that expression, For Old Time's Sake. It was lovely, but I really want to make this work with Lila. It hurts me to hear you say she doesn't love me. I wish you wouldn't say that anymore.

    Besides, I worry about you. I worry that you don't give yourself a chance with anyone else. Like your date that night — Susanah, was that her name? You hardly spoke to her so her name was easy to forget. But she was very pretty and seemed to like you so much, and yet you ignored her. Though you paid more attention, I presume, after you took her back to your room? (Actually, was she old enough to be up that late?)

    Anyway, when next we talk, I want us to be just friends again. Because I do miss your friendship. You can't be my friend if you are angry with me all the time. And you can't stop being angry if we don't understand each other.

                    Yours,
                    H.

When you're humiliated, there's nothing worse than realizing that you have no one to blame but yourself. Shame and fury slammed up against each other inside my head, and yet I felt completely helpless to protest. Had Zena Beth ever made proclamations of love and loyalty to which I could now point with righteous rage? Had she ever behaved as though we were setting up house like Barbie and Ken, Gertrude and Alice, unto eternity? Had she ever led me to think that her love was offered undiluted, without thorny and complicated restrictions?

Still, in love exchanged, there is an unspoken contract. There are certain pleas decent people silently make: don't trample here on this tender place, don't scorch or cut too deeply, don't discard or mock or belittle.

I turned out the light and curled gingerly under the blanket as if the darkness and solitude were a salve against the pain. The sweet and musky scent of her rose off the pillow next to mine and a question, insistent and pleading, came to me: *Could I live with it? Could I?* Because now that I had come this far, how could I live without her?

Sue Havermill and I sat side by side during the crowded council meeting, both of us nearly rigid with impatience for the rest of the business to be done with so that the vote on the gay bill could be taken. She had pointed out Louise Fleck the moment we walked in, but I would have known her anywhere, without any prompting.

To start with, only four of the twelve members were women, and she was the only one in her fifties. Still, even without all that help, I imagined I could have pegged her. She was trim and handsome, her hair short with strict, orderly waves, her black suit blandly conservative. She would have looked right at home at the Swamp Side. How was it that the whole town wasn't onto her? But as always, people manage to see what they want to and can contort even the most objective facts to their own subjective reality when something more important to them is at stake.

As it turned out, I hadn't had to make the tough call about Dotty on my own; she simply didn't pass Ross's veracity test. It was just Dotty's word against Fleck's, he argued — there was not a shred of proof in sight — and Fleck's word would be harder to discredit. In my heart, I believed Dotty completely, but I was relieved to see us not do the interview. It all seemed a sordid business, to punish any woman — even Fleck — for having slept with another, no matter what she said about it the morning after. And I still hoped the fight could be won cleanly and fairly, on principle alone. And if it wasn't, I had my own plans for putting some speed bumps in Fleck's smooth course to continued success.

The town hall was a dark, cavernous space and the twelve councilmembers were up front at a long, mahogany conference table. Rich Richards was seated directly across from Louise Fleck, by design or coincidence, I couldn't know. Sue was covering the story for the T.C., so when I saw her flip open her notebook, I knew they were revving up for the vote.

The chairman, a graying man whose suit was

straining across his stomach, banged his gavel and announced the roll call for Proposition 19, as it was innocuously called. There was no spirited debate, only a grumpy silence broken as each member called out "For" or "Against." They worked their way around the table swiftly, and in the end the vote was two "For" and ten "Against."

Rich Richards was the first to stand and pack up his briefcase, signaling the crowd to disperse. Sue was at his side in seconds, jotting furiously in her pad. Louise Fleck leaned back in her chair leisurely, confident that Sue would get to her next. I hovered nearby, wanting to eavesdrop on the interview.

"Councilmember Fleck, a word with you please?" Sue said, barely even looking up from her pad. Fleck nodded regally. "You campaigned hard against this bill. Do you take credit for its resounding defeat here today?"

"Absolutely not. As you well know, my esteemed colleagues all take pride in well-representing their districts and that's what they did here today in reflecting the community standard."

"You don't see any irony, Councilmember, in a free country where certain communities basically sanction discrimination against gay employees?"

"Irony? No, homosexual marriage does not exist anywhere in this country and in nearly half our states even homosexual sex is still a criminal act. I don't see any logic in asking Mountville to support a highly marginal, largely disapproved of lifestyle with its limited tax dollars."

"What would you say to an employed gay person today who's afraid for his or her job, or who's angry that he won't have the same insurance benefits as his heterosexual co-worker?''

"I would simply say that he or she is enjoying all the rights he's entitled to in this country and county, and that doing one's job to the best of his or her abilities is always the best way to proceed." She smiled tightly and stood up.

Sue, catching sight of a commotion at the other end of the room, dashed away. Louise Fleck didn't notice me standing next to her at first. "Yes, can I help you with something?" she asked, frowning into her briefcase.

"Yes," I said. "I have a message for you from Dotty Oakes." My heart was pounding and my mouth felt cottony but I kept the image of Zena Beth's face in my mind for courage.

Louise Fleck looked up at me casually, but with an awkward jerk of her wrist she sent her pen clattering to the floor. There was still a din in the room but as she and I locked eyes, it was as if the falling pen, rocking back and forth slowly on the tile floor, was the only sound we were registering.

"I don't know any Dotty Oakes. And for that matter, I don't know you."

"Well, there's no reason for you to know me. But it's odd that you don't know Dotty. She's in your district. She's the girls' coach at the high school. I thought you were very involved with the people in your district." I held her eyes till she looked away.

"What of it?"

"She says she remembers your night together fondly and she'd like to do it again sometime."

I smiled sweetly as she gasped, but I didn't hang

around to hear how she would deny it. Denials were, by nature, predictable. Not a single one of them rang true.

Dear Joyce:
  Seattle is, as promised, rainy, but it's also aggressively new. The older I get the more I realize I like a city, like a woman, to have a past. It's just more interesting that way.
  The producers seem like an intelligent group; I feel tentatively confident that they'll do a good job with Dykes. *They're making a big effort to use only out lesbian actresses, which was definitely not an option when it opened in New York all those years ago. Progress. In fact, I've met some of the women and they seem quite up to the parts.*
  I miss you. I'd much rather have you with me but it's some comfort to think of you back at the house, warming the bed, waiting for me. I know I'm not always a comfort to you but we need to find our rhythm with each other yet. We seem to have it down better in some rooms of the house (the bedroom, the bath) better than others.
  If you give me another homecoming like last time I may start to like going away.
                                        Love,
                                        Zena Beth

I retrieved Helena's letter from its place in Zena Beth's phone book and put it in an envelope with the hotel's address. Inside I wrote my own one-line note: "I think you forgot something."

I took it out to the car with me. I wanted to drive to the post office and get it in overnight mail before I lost my nerve.

— 15 —

When I pulled up to the house after work, Zena Beth's Jaguar was in the driveway. She was home a day early. Dread made my legs feel heavy. I bitterly regretted mailing Helena's letter almost as soon as it was out of my hands, but there was nothing to do now but face Zena Beth's anger and disgust.

"Very interesting news in the paper," she said as soon as I was inside the door.

I followed her voice into the living room. Nonchalance — this was a tactic I wouldn't have thought of.

"Welcome home." I hovered in the doorway.

"Very interesting, indeed," Zena Beth said, holding the T.C. out for me to see. "Three insurance companies voluntarily adopt the policy that the defeated gay rights bill would have made mandatory. Very classy." I knew about the story, of course. Sue had written it the night of the vote; I copy edited it. "I even think congratulations are in order."

"No. No, I don't think so," I said, disappointment bitter in my mouth. I had so wanted to make her proud, to make her feel I was worthy of joining in the work she was trying to do.

I sat down on the chair across from her, my whole body tensed. Seeing her, her hair windblown, her cheeks freshly pink from outdoors, I felt the hunger for her begin. A hunger that, this time, might go unsatisfied.

"Why not? You're quite the detective, aren't you? I'm glad to see you didn't retire your newspaper skills so soon after you learned them."

I flinched. I couldn't have felt more threatened if she had been holding a bat poised at my head. "I was looking for Dotty's phone number. The letter fluttered out. I'm human."

"Well, so am I, it would seem." She smiled cruelly. "Shall we call it even, then?"

I stared; she was serious. "You don't really mean you see these as transgressions of equal weight?"

"No, I don't. You're right." She crossed her legs at the ankle. "Your betrayal is far worse."

Fear vibrated inside me like a tuning fork. I wasn't up to this, a fight this ugly with Zena Beth Frazer. I was no match for her hostility when the only defense I had was the pain of a wounded lover.

"If that's what you really think," I said finally, "we have less in common than I thought."

"I never withheld anything from you because of my other involvements. Maybe you imagine I'd be a different kind of lover if there was absolutely no one else, ever, but you're wrong. I'm giving you everything I can give you."

I searched her face and decided she was telling the truth. It was more frightening than any lie she might have manufactured.

"But what you did," she went on, "was prove yourself untrustworthy in the most profound way."

My temples and upper lip grew damp. She nearly had me convinced. "No, what I did was unfortunate. And maybe it was a little desperate. But it was also an act of hope. I hoped I might find out more about you, or how you felt about me."

I stood up and began to pace. "Yes, I'm an adult, you can ask me down here and that doesn't make you responsible for my life. But you might have had a hunch what I was thinking, leaving behind everything I had and knew. You might have figured that I expected you were giving up some things, too. If not old loves, then for God's sake new ones, random ones. What good do they do you, anyway — except to give you a moment like this, when you can hold us all at arm's length?"

"Oh, don't psychoanalyze. It's tedious." She looked away, out the window.

I bit my bottom lip, willing myself with all my strength not to cry. But it was torture to see her close enough to embrace, and yet so completely out of reach. "Don't you ever think there are some things you can say that are unforgivable?"

"It's not me who's done the unforgivable."

"Ah," I said, "so it's not your deceit that's the crime. It's mine for being tacky enough to say I noticed."

"Look," she said, her voice steely with anger. "I'm not interested in pinning blame. But I need to know that my privacy is sacred, or I can't trust you. I'm sorry if my scope of privacy reaches further than you think it should. If you can adjust to that, we can go on. I'm not giving you half or thirds of anything that's yours. You get all of what I feel for you."

"Well, you must be awfully big-hearted, then, with so much affection to go around."

She stood up. "Let's not do this." She shook her head. "I'm out of energy for scenes like this."

"And in your fantasy, then, everything goes well all of the time?" I watched her but she wouldn't look up. "Is that it?"

"I need to unpack," she said as she walked by me up the stairs.

And what I needed, I supposed, was to pack.

I had never been to Luce's place before, and it was just lucky that I found her home. She answered the door in a smock covered with paint and clay smears.

"I'm sorry to bother you while you're working," I said. "But I —"

"No bother at all. Come in." She stepped aside, wiping wet clay off her fingers with a cloth, searching my face, I guessed, to gauge my mood and purpose. "Let me show you the studio while you're here. I've been meaning to do that, actually, but I never got up the — I mean, I never quite got around to it."

She led us downstairs to a cool basement rich with the smell of clay and wood. Against one wall floor-to-ceiling shelves held pots and vases in various stages of completion — some fired and painted, some still raw and uneven. On a wheel in the middle of the room was a large bowl, still dripping and ringed with fingermarks.

"It's great. It feels very much like you," I said.

"Well," she said, looking around happily, "I'm very comfortable here. Very relaxed. Speaking of which, can I get you a drink or something?"

I waited in the living room while she put up coffee. Her house was much smaller than Zena Beth's, but cozy, decorated with quilts and wall hangings, striking and unmatched pieces of pottery and statues.

She came in, without her smock, and handed me a mug. "So, to what do I owe this pleasure?" She sat down cross-legged on the couch across from me.

I stalled, sipping the coffee. Maybe I was putting her in an awkward position. "I have no one else to talk to, Luce."

"Don't apologize." She ran a hand through her silver-streaked hair. "I'm glad I can help."

"Do you think I'm crazy? I want the whole thing. I don't want just part of her attention. I'm afraid —" My voice cracked and I stopped.

"It's okay," Luce said, coming over to sit next to me. "Get it out."

"I'm afraid it won't get better than this. That she won't grow to love me more. I was counting on that all along." My face was hot. "I feel like — like she needs an audience all the time. And that's just what I am. A deeply appreciative audience."

"What happened, exactly?" Luce asked quietly.

"I'm so stupid, really," I said. "I knew it all along about Helena. I mean, I guess I didn't think she still slept with her whenever she could, but that's just a detail, isn't it? Everyone knows she's still in love with her. It's the others I didn't know about. If it wasn't me waiting in the hotel room, it was some other adoring fan. Is that what I have to do? Follow her all around the country if I want fidelity? Do you think I'm pathetically old-fashioned?"

Luce frowned into her coffee mug and pursed her lips. "No," she whispered. "It's partly my fault. I should have warned you. I know how she is. On one hand, she doesn't have much use for most people, and on the other, she can't bear to be alone. I should have told you."

"Oh, so everyone knew, huh? No, it's not your fault," I said, when I saw how stricken she looked. "I'd never have expected you to tell me. That wasn't your place. It was hers, only hers."

"I *don't* think you're crazy," she said, pressing my shoulder. "But believe me, you don't want her consumed with you, either. Everyone saw how she was with Helena. It was a suffocating kind of love. It was ferocious. There was no escaping it."

I studied Luce's face. Maybe she knew firsthand. Maybe that was how Zena Beth had been with her when they were much younger, before the world was in love with Zena Beth Frazer and she could have any woman she wanted. "You've been a friend all the way along, Luce."

"No, not really. Because I've been partly pretending." She put her mug down. "I've wanted to be . . . more."

She looked at me for a moment, then leaned forward and touched her lips lightly to mine, light as a firefly landing, soft as a gulf breeze blowing.

Delight welled up in me, but I couldn't respond. Part of the joy would be in hurting Zena Beth — sleeping with her best friend — and Luce deserved better.

"I'm very tempted," I said, slowly pulling back, "but I have to go home. To New York, I mean. There's someone there I . . . some unfinished business." I stood up, not wanting to make the moment any more awkward for her than it had to be.

"Say no more." She stood up resignedly and walked me to the door. "Look," she said, "if you change your mind about Zena Beth when you get back there, if you decide you can make compromises, I won't lose respect for you." She smiled. "She's a very persuasive woman. And a lot of women feel she's worth compromising for."

When I got back, the house was dark and the Jaguar was nowhere in sight. Panic made my heart clatter in my throat. Was I crazy for thinking that I could just walk away from her when I was frantic at the idea of not being with her tonight? I ran up the stairs to the bedroom.

Dear Joyce, the letter on my pillow began.

   Yes, I suppose in my fantasy everything does go exactly right all the time. In a fantasy, you'd be crazy to have it any other way, wouldn't you?
   And if things went right all the time, you'd fall in love only with people who loved you back with equal intensity, and in just the same way. Not as a friend when you loved them as a lover. Or not as a playmate when you loved them as your most serious undertaking ever.
   Unfortunately, that's life's central torture: We love people who aren't worthy of us. Or we love people who haven't the slightest idea who we really are. Or we love people who feel things for us that, when we're in love, are worse than contempt — they are fond of us or think we're fun and amusing.
   And if things went right all the time, when we saw someone who loved us with every worthwhile fiber of her heart and soul, we'd match her love ... and then some, if we could bear it. Instead, all we can do is nurse the spark and guard it and rejoice at all the times it bursts into flames.
   Because I have been on fire with you, Joyce. Be patient with me. I wish you could be patient.

                                        Love,
                                        Zena Beth

I turned the light back off and lay down and waited.

I stayed the rest of the summer.

It was not a summer to be proud of. Luce was right about a lot of things. I compromised. And pride matters.

Zena Beth would have gone on like that indefinitely, I think (or maybe I'm still kidding myself) but in my mind a love affair is like a river. It ought to get deeper as it goes, or spill over waterfalls or irrigate the land. Instead, ours just seeped into a pond and stood still. At least I have that now — country metaphors. It was something I didn't have before.

Every once in a while she comes up to New York. To sign a new collection of one-act plays. To read at the West Side Y. To be a guest lecturer at the New School. More than once I went. I never told Elaine — our getting back together was too fresh, too tentative, and ultimately too precious.

When I went, I sat in the audience and listened. I felt scalded watching her address so many people; it was like bursting in on her in bed with another woman. How could she belong to all these people at the same time when she had once been just mine? When I couldn't bear it, I shut my eyes and let her voice wash over me, felt the press of it, the warmth of it, against my ear, heard her making all the sweet promises she had once made, imagined her making others she had never managed.

Once she spotted me at the back of the room as I was filing out with the crowd. She called out my name over all the heads in the room, and the sound was as intimate as a caress. People craned around jealously to see who had been fingered for special favor. She was friendly and cordial, interested even, and everyone smiled on, without a clue about why the exchange was intolerable to me. I could have borne her hostility more than her politeness. Passion is passion. I made sure she never spotted me again, and finally I just stopped going.

I did wait. I am a patient woman. What I waited for, though, was her to wear off. Or maybe I was waiting to become somebody she'd admire as much as I admired her, or to become somebody *I* admired as much as I admired her.

I did go back to the paper, but not as a staffer — my old job had long been filled and there were no other openings. But I wrote for them, and other places, whenever I could, and even though it was scary as hell not to have a paycheck coming in regularly, I felt I was getting to say something, getting to pick and pursue stories that mattered to me. And people were starting to know my byline and what it stood for. I always hoped that somehow Zena Beth saw the stories but I never sent them to her myself.

Luce was good about sending postcards and I even bought a piece of her pottery for Nikki and Caryn as a moving-in-together present. But as if by some unspoken pact, she never mentioned Zena Beth, and we both preferred it that way.

I still have the tissue with her lipstick mark. And I still have her letters, all of them. I can nearly recite them, feel the cadence of their sentences, the weight of each word. I've imagined her at the desks in her hotel rooms as she might have been as she wrote them. I've imagined her as she signed, "Love, Zena Beth." And I do. And always will.